The Big Sleep

RAYMOND CHANDLER

The Big Sleep

PENGUIN BOOKS

PENGUIN CLASSICS

Published by the Penguin Group
Penguin Books Ltd, 80 Strand, London WC2R 0RL, England
Penguin Group (USA) Inc., 375 Hudson Street, New York, New York 10014, USA
Penguin Group (Canada), 90 Eglinton Avenue East, Suite 700, Toronto, Ontario, Canada M4P 2Y3
(a division of Pearson Penguin Canada Inc.)
Penguin Ireland, 25 St Stephen's Green, Dublin 2, Ireland (a division of Penguin Books Ltd)
Penguin Group (Australia), 250 Camberwell Road, Camberwell, Victoria 3124, Australia
(a division of Pearson Australia Group Pty Ltd)
Penguin Books India Pvt Ltd, 11 Community Centre, Panchsheel Park, New Delhi – 110 017, India
Penguin Group (NZ), 67 Apollo Drive, Rosedale, North Shore 0632, New Zealand
(a division of Pearson New Zealand Ltd)
Penguin Books (South Africa) (Pty) Ltd, 24 Sturdee Avenue,
Rosebank, Johannesburg 2196, South Africa

Penguin Books Ltd, Registered Offices: 80 Strand, London WC2R 0RL, England

www.penguin.com

First published in Great Britain by Hamish Hamilton 1939
This edition published 2009
1

Set in 12/14 pt Monotype Perpetua
Typeset by Rowland Phototypesetting Ltd, Bury St Edmunds, Suffolk
Printed in England by Clays Ltd, St Ives plc

978-0-141-19315-1

I

It was about eleven o'clock in the morning, mid October, with the sun not shining and a look of hard wet rain in the clearness of the foothills. I was wearing my powder-blue suit, with dark blue shirt, tie and display handkerchief, black brogues, black wool socks with dark blue clocks on them. I was neat, clean, shaved and sober, and I didn't care who knew it. I was everything the well-dressed private detective ought to be. I was calling on four million dollars.

The main hallway of the Sternwood place was two storeys high. Over the entrance doors, which would have let in a troop of Indian elephants, there was a broad stained-glass panel showing a knight in dark armour rescuing a lady who was tied to a tree and didn't have any clothes on but some very long and convenient hair. The knight had pushed the vizor of his helmet back to be sociable, and he was fiddling with the knots on the ropes that tied the lady to the tree and not getting anywhere. I stood there and thought that if I lived in the house, I would sooner or later have to climb up there and help him. He didn't seem to be really trying.

There were French doors at the back of the hall, beyond them a wide sweep of emerald grass to a white garage, in front of which a slim dark young chauffeur in shiny black leggings was dusting a maroon Packard convertible. Beyond the garage were some decorative trees trimmed as carefully as poodle dogs. Beyond them a large greenhouse with a domed roof. Then more trees and beyond everything the solid, uneven, comfortable line of the foothills.

On the east side of the hall a free staircase, tile-paved, rose to a gallery with a wrought-iron railing and another piece of stained-glass romance. Large hard chairs with rounded red plush seats were backed into the vacant spaces of the wall round about. They didn't look as if anybody had ever sat in them. In the middle of the west wall there was a big empty fireplace with a brass screen in four hinged panels, and over the fireplace a marble mantel with cupids at the corners. Above the mantel there was a large oil portrait, and above the portrait two bullet-torn or moth-eaten cavalry pennants crossed in a glass frame. The portrait was a stiffly posed job of an officer in full regimentals of about the time of the Mexican War. The officer had a neat black imperial, black mustachios, hot hard coal-black eyes, and the general look of a man it would pay to get along with. I thought this might be General Sternwood's grandfather. It could hardly be the General himself, even though I had heard he was pretty far gone in years to have a couple of daughters still in the dangerous twenties.

I was still staring at the hot black eyes when a door

opened far back under the stairs. It wasn't the butler coming back. It was a girl.

She was twenty or so, small and delicately put together, but she looked durable. She wore pale blue slacks and they looked well on her. She walked as if she were floating. Her hair was a fine tawny wave cut much shorter than the current fashion of pageboy tresses curled in at the bottom. Her eyes were slate-grey, and had almost no expression when they looked at me. She came over near me and smiled with her mouth and she had little sharp predatory teeth, as white as fresh orange pith and as shiny as porcelain. They glistened between her thin too taut lips. Her face lacked colour and didn't look too healthy.

'Tall, aren't you?' she said.

'I didn't mean to be.'

Her eyes rounded. She was puzzled. She was thinking. I could see, even on that short acquaintance, that thinking was always going to be a bother to her.

'Handsome too,' she said. 'And I bet you know it.'

I grunted.

'What's your name?'

'Reilly,' I said. 'Doghouse Reilly.'

'That's a funny name.' She bit her lip and turned her head a little and looked at me along her eyes. Then she lowered her lashes until they almost cuddled her cheeks and slowly raised them again, like a theatre curtain. I was to get to know that trick. That was supposed to make me roll over on my back with all four paws in the air.

'Are you a prizefighter?' she asked, when I didn't.

'Not exactly. I'm a sleuth.'

'A–a–' She tossed her head angrily, and the rich colour of it glistened in the rather dim light of the big hall. 'You're making fun of me.'

'Uh-uh.'

'What?'

'Get on with you,' I said. 'You heard me.'

'You didn't say anything. You're just a big tease.' She put a thumb up and bit it. It was a curiously shaped thumb, thin and narrow like an extra finger, with no curve in the first joint. She bit it and sucked it slowly, turning it around in her mouth like a baby with a comforter.

'You're awfully tall,' she said. Then she giggled with secret merriment. Then she turned her body slowly and lithely, without lifting her feet. Her hands dropped limp at her sides. She tilted herself towards me on her toes. She fell straight back into my arms. I had to catch her or let her crack her head on the tessellated floor. I caught her under her arms and she went rubber-legged on me instantly. I had to hold her close to hold her up. When her head was against my chest she screwed it around and giggled at me.

'You're cute,' she giggled. 'I'm cute too.'

I didn't say anything. So the butler chose that convenient moment to come back through the French doors and see me holding her.

It didn't seem to bother him. He was a tall thin silver man, sixty or close to it or a little past it. He had blue eyes as remote as eyes could be. His skin was smooth and bright and he moved like a man with very sound muscles. He walked slowly across the floor towards us and the girl jerked away from me. She flashed across the room to the foot of the stairs and went up them like a deer. She was gone before I could draw a long breath and let it out.

The butler said tonelessly: 'The General will see you now, Mr Marlowe.'

I pushed my lower jaw up off my chest and nodded at him. 'Who was that?'

'Miss Carmen Sternwood, sir.'

'You ought to wean her. She looks old enough.'

He looked at me with grave politeness and repeated what he had said.

2

We went out at the French doors and along a smooth red-flagged path that skirted the far side of the lawn from the garage. The boyish-looking chauffeur had a big black and chromium sedan out now and was dusting that. The path took us along to the side of the greenhouse and the butler opened a door for me and stood aside. It opened into a sort of vestibule that was about as warm as a slow oven. He came in after me, shut the outer door, opened an inner door and we went through that. Then it was really hot. The air was thick, wet, steamy and larded with the cloying smell of tropical orchids in bloom. The glass walls and roof were heavily misted and big drops of moisture splashed down on the plants. The light had an unreal greenish colour, like light filtered through an aquarium tank. The plants filled the place, a forest of them, with nasty meaty leaves and stalks like the newly washed fingers of dead men. They smelled as overpowering as boiling alcohol under a blanket.

The butler did his best to get me through without being smacked in the face by the sodden leaves, and after a while we came to a clearing in the middle of the jungle, under the domed roof. Here, in a space of hexagonal flags, an old red Turkish rug was laid down and on the rug was a wheel chair, and in the wheel chair an old and obviously dying man watched us come with black eyes from which all fire had died long ago, but which still had the coal-black directness of the eyes in the portrait that hung above the mantel in the hall. The rest of his face was a leaden mask, with the bloodless lips and the sharp nose and the sunken temples and the outward-turning ear-lobes of approaching dissolution. His long narrow body was wrapped – in that heat – in a travelling rug and a faded red bathrobe. His thin clawlike hands were folded loosely on the rug, purple-nailed. A few locks of dry white hair clung to his scalp, like wild flowers fighting for life on a bare rock.

The butler stood in front of him and said: 'This is Mr Marlowe, General.'

The old man didn't move or speak, or even nod. He just looked at me lifelessly. The butler pushed a damp wicker chair against the backs of my legs and I sat down. He took my hat with a deft scoop.

Then the old man dragged his voice up from the bottom of a well and said: 'Brandy, Norris. How do you like your brandy, sir?'

'Any way at all,' I said.

The butler went away among the abominable plants. The General spoke again, slowly, using his strength as carefully as an out-of-work showgirl uses her last good pair of stockings.

'I used to like mine with champagne. The champagne as cold as Valley Forge and about a third of a glass of brandy beneath it. You may take your coat off, sir. It's too hot in here for a man with blood in his veins.'

I stood up and peeled off my coat and got a handkerchief out and mopped my face and neck and the backs of my wrists. St Louis in August had nothing on that place. I sat down again and felt automatically for a cigarette and then stopped. The old man caught the gesture and smiled faintly.

'You may smoke, sir. I like the smell of tobacco.'

I lit the cigarette and blew a lungful at him and he sniffed at it like a terrier at a rat-hole. The faint smile pulled at the shadowed corners of his mouth.

'A nice state of affairs when a man has to indulge his vices by proxy,' he said dryly. 'You are looking at a very dull survival of a rather gaudy life, a cripple paralysed in both legs and with only half of his lower belly. There's very little that I can eat and my sleep is so close to waking that it is hardly worth the name. I seem to exist largely on heat, like a newborn spider, and the orchids are an excuse for the heat. Do you like orchids?'

'Not particularly,' I said.

The General half closed his eyes. 'They are nasty things. Their flesh is too much like the flesh of men. And their perfume has the rotten sweetness of a prostitute.'

I stared at him with my mouth open. The soft wet heat was like a pall around us. The old man nodded, as if his neck was afraid of the weight of his head. Then the butler came pushing back through the jungle with a tea-wagon, mixed me a brandy and soda, swathed the copper ice bucket with a damp napkin, and went softly away among the orchids. A door opened and shut behind the jungle.

I sipped the drink. The old man licked his lips watching me, over and over again, drawing one lip slowly across the other with a funereal absorption, like an undertaker dry-washing his hands.

'Tell me about yourself, Mr Marlowe. I suppose I have a right to ask?'

'Sure, but there's very little to tell. I'm thirty-three years old, went to college once and can still speak English if there's any demand for it. There isn't much in my trade. I worked for Mr Wilde, the District Attorney, as an investigator once. His chief investigator, a man named Bernie Ohls, called me and told me you wanted to see me. I'm unmarried because I don't like policemen's wives.'

'And a little bit of a cynic,' the old man smiled. 'You didn't like working for Wilde?'

'I was fired. For insubordination. I test very high on insubordination, General.'

'I always did myself, sir. I'm glad to hear it. What do you know about my family?'

'I'm told you are a widower and have two young daughters, both pretty and both wild. One of them has been married three times, the last time to an ex-bootlegger, who went in the trade by the name of Rusty Regan. That's all I heard, General.'

'Did any of it strike you as peculiar?'

'The Rusty Regan part, maybe. But I always got along with bootleggers myself.'

He smiled his faint economical smile. 'It seems I do too. I'm very fond of Rusty. A big curly-headed Irishman from Clonmel, with sad eyes and a smile as wide as

Wilshire Boulevard. The first time I saw him I thought he might be what you are probably thinking he was, an adventurer who happened to get himself wrapped up in some velvet.'

'You must have liked him,' I said. 'You learned to talk the language.'

He put his thin bloodless hands under the edge of the rug. I put my cigarette stub out and finished my drink.

'He was the breath of life to me – while he lasted. He spent hours with me, sweating like a pig, drinking brandy by the quart, and telling me stories of the Irish revolution. He had been an officer in the IRA. He wasn't even legally in the United States. It was a ridiculous marriage of course, and it probably didn't last a month, as a marriage. I'm telling you the family secrets, Mr Marlowe.'

'They're still secrets,' I said. 'What happened to him?'

The old man looked at me woodenly. 'He went away, a month ago. Abruptly, without a word to anyone. Without saying good-bye to me. That hurt a little, but he had been raised in a rough school. I'll hear from him one of these days. Meantime I am being blackmailed again.'

I said: 'Again?'

He brought his hands from under the rug with a brown envelope in them. 'I should have been very sorry for anybody who tried to blackmail me while Rusty was around. A few months before he came – that is to say about nine or ten months ago – I paid a man named Joe Brody five thousand dollars to let my younger daughter Carmen alone.'

'Ah,' I said.

He moved his thin white eyebrows. 'That means what?'

'Nothing,' I said.

He went on staring at me, half frowning. Then he said: 'Take this envelope and examine it. And help yourself to the brandy.'

I took the envelope off his knees and sat down with it again. I wiped off the palms of my hands and turned it around. It was addressed to General Guy Sternwood, 3765 Alta Brea Crescent, West Hollywood, California. The address was in ink, in the slanting printing engineers use. The envelope was slit. I opened it up and took out a brown card and three slips of stiff paper. The card was of thin brown linen, printed in gold: 'Mr Arthur Gwynn Geiger.' No address. Very small in the lower lefthand corner: 'Rare Books and De Luxe Editions.' I turned the card over. More of the slanted printing on the back. 'Dear Sir: In spite of the legal uncollectibility of the enclosed, which frankly represent gambling debts, I assume you might wish them honoured. Respectfully, A. G. Geiger.'

I looked at the slips of stiffish white paper. They were promissory notes filled out in ink, dated on several dates early in the month before, September. 'On Demand I promise to pay to Arthur Gwynn Geiger or Order the sum of One Thousand Dollars ($1000.00) without interest. Value Received. Carmen Sternwood.'

The written part was in a sprawling moronic handwriting with a lot of fat curlicues and circles for dots. I mixed myself another drink and sipped it and put the exhibit aside.

'Your conclusions?' the General asked.

'I haven't any yet. Who is this Arthur Gwynn Geiger?'

'I haven't the faintest idea.'

'What does Carmen say?'

'I haven't asked her. I don't intend to. If I did, she would suck her thumb and look coy.'

I said: 'I met her in the hall. She did that to me. Then she tried to sit in my lap.'

Nothing changed in his expression. His clasped hands rested peacefully on the edge of the rug, and the heat, which made me feel like a New England boiled dinner, didn't seem to make him even warm.

'Do I have to be polite?' I asked. 'Or can I just be natural?'

'I haven't noticed that you suffer from many inhibitions, Mr Marlowe.'

'Do the two girls run around together?'

'I think not. I think they go their separate and slightly divergent roads to perdition. Vivian is spoiled, exacting, smart and quite ruthless. Carmen is a child who likes to pull wings off flies. Neither of them has any more moral sense than a cat. Neither have I. No Sternwood ever had. Proceed.'

'They're well educated, I suppose. They know what they're doing.'

'Vivian went to good schools of the snob type and to college. Carmen went to half a dozen schools of greater and greater liberality, and ended up where she started. I presume they both had, and still have, all the usual vices. If I sound a little sinister as a parent, Mr Marlowe, it is because my hold on life is too slight to include any

Victorian hypocrisy.' He leaned his head back and closed his eyes, then opened them again suddenly. 'I need not add that a man who indulges in parenthood for the first time at the age of fifty-four deserves all he gets.'

I sipped my drink and nodded. The pulse in his lean grey throat throbbed visibly and yet so slowly that it was hardly a pulse at all. An old man two-thirds dead and still determined to believe he could take it.

'Your conclusions?' he asked suddenly.

'I'd pay him.'

'Why?'

'It's a question of a little money against a lot of annoyance. There has to be something behind it. But nobody's going to break your heart, if it hasn't been done already. And it would take an awful lot of chisellers an awful lot of time to rob you of enough so that you'd even notice it.'

'I have pride, sir,' he said coldly.

'Somebody's counting on that. It's the easiest way to fool them. That or the police. Geiger can collect on these notes, unless you can show fraud. Instead of that he makes you a present of them and admits they are gambling debts, which gives you a defence, even if he had kept the notes. If he's a crook, he knows his onions, and if he's an honest man doing a little loan business on the side, he ought to have his money. Who was this Joe Brody you paid the five thousand dollars to?'

'Some kind of gambler. I hardly recall. Norris would know. My butler.'

'Your daughters have money in their own right, General?'

'Vivian has, but not a great deal. Carmen is still a minor under her mother's will. I give them both generous allowances.'

I said: 'I can take this Geiger off your back, General, if that's what you want. Whoever he is and whatever he has. It may cost you a little money, besides what you pay me. And, of course, it won't get you anything. Sugaring them never does. You're already listed on their book of nice names.'

'I see.' He shrugged his wide sharp shoulders in the faded red bathrobe. 'A moment ago you said pay him. Now you say it won't get me anything.'

'I mean it might be cheaper and easier to stand for a certain amount of squeeze. That's all.'

'I'm afraid I'm rather an impatient man, Mr Marlowe. What are your charges?'

'I get twenty-five a day and expenses – when I'm lucky.'

'I see. It seems reasonable enough for removing morbid growths from people's backs. Quite a delicate operation. You realize that, I hope. You'll make your operation as little of a shock to the patient as possible? There might be several of them, Mr Marlowe.'

I finished my second drink and wiped my lips and my face. The heat didn't get any less hot with the brandy in me. The General blinked at me and plucked at the edge of his rug.

'Can I make a deal with this guy, if I think he's within hooting distance of being on the level?'

'Yes. The matter is now in your hands. I never do things by halves.'

'I'll take him out,' I said. 'He'll think a bridge fell on him.'

'I'm sure you will. And now I must excuse myself. I am tired.' He reached out and touched the bell on the arm of his chair. The cord was plugged into a black cable that wound along the side of the deep dark green boxes in which the orchids grew and festered. He closed his eyes, opened them again in a brief bright stare, and settled back among his cushions. The lids dropped again and he didn't pay any more attention to me.

I stood up and lifted my coat off the back of the damp wicker chair and went off with it among the orchids, opened the two doors and stood outside in the brisk October air getting myself some oxygen. The chauffeur over by the garage had gone away. The butler came along the red path with smooth light steps and his back as straight as an ironing board. I shrugged into my coat and watched him come.

He stopped about two feet from me and said gravely: 'Mrs Regan would like to see you before you leave, sir. And in the matter of money the General has instructed me to give you a cheque for whatever seems desirable.'

'Instructed you how?'

He looked puzzled, then he smiled. 'Ah, I see, sir. You are, of course, a detective. By the way he rang his bell.'

'You write his cheques?'

'I have that privilege.'

'That ought to save you from a pauper's grave. No money now, thanks. What does Mrs Regan want to see me about?'

His blue eyes gave me a smooth level look. 'She has a misconception of the purpose of your visit, sir.'

'Who told her anything about my visit?'

'Her windows command the greenhouse. She saw us go in. I was obliged to tell her who you were.'

'I don't like that,' I said.

His blue eyes frosted. 'Are you attempting to tell me my duties, sir?'

'No. But I'm having a lot of fun trying to guess what they are.'

We stared at each other for a moment. He gave me a blue glare and turned away.

3

This room was too big, the ceiling was too high, the doors were too tall, and the white carpet that went from wall to wall looked like a fresh fall of snow at Lake Arrowhead. There were full-length mirrors and crystal doodads all over the place. The ivory furniture had chromium on it, and the enormous ivory drapes lay tumbled on the white carpet a yard from the windows. The white made the ivory look dirty and the ivory made the white look bled out. The windows stared towards the darkening foothills. It was going to rain soon. There was pressure in the air already.

I sat down on the edge of a deep soft chair and looked at Mrs Regan. She was worth a stare. She was trouble. She was stretched out on a modernistic chaise-longue with her slippers off, so I stared at her legs in the sheerest silk stockings. They seemed to be arranged to stare at. They were visible to the knee and one of them well beyond. The knees were dimpled, not bony and sharp. The calves were beautiful, the ankles long and slim and with enough melodic line for a tone poem. She was tall and rangy and strong-looking. Her head was against an ivory satin cushion. Her hair was black and wiry and parted in the middle and she had the hot black eyes of the portrait in the hall. She had a good mouth and a good chin. There was a sulky droop to her lips and the lower lip was full.

She had a drink. She took a swallow from it and gave me a cool level stare over the rim of the glass.

'So you're a private detective,' she said. 'I didn't know they really existed, except in books. Or else they were greasy little men snooping around hotels.'

There was nothing in that for me, so I let it drift with the current. She put her glass down on the flat arm of the chaise-longue and flashed an emerald and touched her hair. She said slowly: 'How did you like Dad?'

'I liked him,' I said.

'He liked Rusty. I suppose you know who Rusty is?'

'Uh-huh.'

'Rusty was earthy and vulgar at times, but he was very real. And he was a lot of fun for Dad. Rusty shouldn't have gone off like that. Dad feels very badly about it, although he won't say so. Or did he?'

'He said something about it.'

'You're not much of a gusher, are you, Mr Marlowe? But he wants to find him, doesn't he?'

I stared at her politely through a pause. 'Yes and no,' I said.

'That's hardly an answer. Do you think you can find him?'

'I didn't say I was going to try. Why not try the Missing Persons Bureau? They have the organization. It's not a one-man job.'

'Oh, Dad wouldn't hear of the police being brought

into it.' She looked at me smoothly across her glass again, emptied it, and rang a bell. A maid came into the room by a side door. She was a middle-aged woman with a long yellow gentle face, a long nose, no chin, large wet eyes. She looked like a nice old horse that had been turned out to pasture after long service. Mrs Regan waved the empty glass at her and she mixed another drink and handed it to her and left the room, without a word, without a glance in my direction.

When the door shut Mrs Regan said: 'Well, how will you go about it then?'

'How and when did he skip out?'

'Didn't Dad tell you?'

I grinned at her with my head on one side. She flushed. Her hot black eyes looked mad. 'I don't see what there is to be cagey about,' she snapped. 'And I don't like your manners.'

'I'm not crazy about yours,' I said. 'I didn't ask to see you. You sent for me. I don't mind your ritzing me or drinking your lunch out of a Scotch bottle. I don't mind your showing me your legs. They're very swell legs and it's a pleasure to make their acquaintance. I don't mind if you don't like my manners. They're pretty bad. I grieve over them during the long winter evenings. But don't waste your time trying to cross-examine me.'

She slammed her glass down so hard that it slopped over on an ivory cushion. She swung her legs to the floor and stood up with her eyes sparking fire and her nostrils wide. Her mouth was open and her bright teeth glared at me. Her knuckles were white.

'People don't talk like that to me,' she said thickly.

I sat there and grinned at her. Very slowly she closed her mouth and looked down at the spilled liquor. She sat down on the edge of the chaise-longue and cupped her chin in one hand.

'My God, you big dark handsome brute! I ought to throw a Buick at you.'

I snicked a match on my thumbnail and for once it lit. I puffed smoke into the air and waited.

'I loathe masterful men,' she said. 'I simply loathe them.'

'Just what is it you're afraid of, Mrs Regan?'

Her eyes whitened. Then they darkened until they seemed to be all pupil. Her nostrils looked pinched.

'That wasn't what he wanted with you at all,' she said in a strained voice that still had shreds of anger clinging to it. 'About Rusty. Was it?'

'Better ask him.'

She flared up again. 'Get out! Damn you, get out!'

I stood up. 'Sit down!' she snapped. I sat down. I flicked a finger at my palm and waited.

'Please,' she said. 'Please. You could find Rusty – if Dad wanted you to.'

That didn't work either. I nodded and asked: 'When did he go?'

'One afternoon a month back. He just drove away in his car without saying a word. They found the car in a private garage somewhere.'

'They?'

She got cunning. Her whole body seemed to go lax.

Then she smiled at me winningly. 'He didn't tell you then.' Her voice was almost gleeful, as if she had outsmarted me. Maybe she had.

'He told me about Mr Regan, yes. That's not what he wanted to see me about. Is that what you've been trying to get me to say?'

'I'm sure I don't care what you say.'

I stood up again. 'Then I'll be running along.' She didn't speak. I went over to the tall white door I had come in at. When I looked back she had her lip between her teeth and was worrying it like a puppy at the fringe of a rug.

I went out, down the tile staircase to the hall, and the butler drifted out of somewhere with my hat in his hand. I put it on while he opened the door for me.

'You made a mistake,' I said. 'Mrs Regan didn't want to see me.'

He inclined his silver head and said politely: 'I'm sorry, sir. I make many mistakes.' He closed the door against my back.

I stood on the step breathing my cigarette smoke and looking down a succession of terraces with flowerbeds and trimmed trees to the high iron fence with gilt spears that hemmed in the estate. A winding driveway dropped down between retaining walls to the open iron gates. Beyond the fence the hill sloped for several miles. On this lower level faint and far off I could just barely see some of the old wooden derricks of the oilfield from which the Sternwoods had made their money. Most of the field was public park now, cleaned up and donated to the city by

General Sternwood. But a little of it was still producing in groups of wells pumping five or six barrels a day. The Sternwoods, having moved up the hill, could no longer smell the stale sump water or the oil, but they could still look out of their front windows and see what had made them rich. If they wanted to. I don't suppose they would want to.

I walked down a brick path from terrace to terrace, followed along inside the fence and so out of the gates to where I had left my car under a pepper tree on the street. Thunder was crackling in the foothills now and the sky above them was purple-black. It was going to rain hard. The air had the damp foretaste of rain. I put the top up on my convertible before I started down-town.

She had lovely legs. I would say that for her. They were a couple of pretty smooth citizens, she and her father. He was probably just trying me out; the job he had given me was a lawyer's job. Even if Mr Arthur Gwynn Geiger, *Rare Books and De Luxe Editions*, turned out to be a blackmailer, it was still a lawyer's job. Unless there was a lot more to it than met the eye. At a casual glance I thought I might have a lot of fun finding out.

I drove down to the Hollywood public library and did a little superficial research in a stuffy volume called *Famous First Editions*. Half an hour of it made me need my lunch.

4

A. G. Geiger's place was a store frontage on the north side of the boulevard near Las Palmas. The entrance door was set far back in the middle and there was a copper trim on the windows, which were backed with Chinese screens, so I couldn't see into the store. There was a lot of oriental junk in the windows. I didn't know whether it was any good, not being a collector of antiques, except unpaid bills. The entrance door was plate glass, but I couldn't see much through that either, because the store was very dim. A building entrance adjoined it on one side and on the other was a glittering credit jewellery establishment. The jeweller stood in his entrance, teetering on his heels and looking bored, a tall handsome white-haired Jew in lean dark clothes, with about nine carats of diamond on his right hand. A faint knowing smile curved his lips when I turned into Geiger's store. I let the door close softly behind me and walked on a thick blue rug that paved the floor from wall to wall. There were blue leather easy chairs with smoke stands beside them. A few sets of tooled leather bindings were set out on narrow polished tables, between book ends. There were more tooled bindings in glass cases on the walls. Nice-looking merchandise, the kind a rich promoter would buy by the yard and have somebody paste his book-plate in. At the back there was a grained wood partition with a door in the middle of it, shut. In the corner made by the partition and one wall a woman sat behind a small desk with a carved wooden lantern on it.

She got up slowly and swayed towards me in a tight black dress that didn't reflect any light. She had long thighs and she walked with a certain something I hadn't often seen in bookstores. She was an ash blonde with greenish eyes, beaded lashes, hair waved smoothly back from ears in which large jet buttons glittered. Her fingernails were silvered. In spite of her get-up she looked as if she would have a hall bedroom accent.

She approached me with enough sex appeal to stampede a businessmen's lunch and tilted her head to finger a stray, but not very stray, tendril of softly glowing hair. Her smile was tentative, but could be persuaded to be nice.

'Was it something?' she inquired.

I had my horn-rimmed sun-glasses on. I put my voice high and let a bird twitter in it. 'Would you happen to have a *Ben Hur* 1860?'

She didn't say: 'Huh?' but she wanted to. She smiled bleakly. 'A first edition?'

'Third,' I said. 'The one with the erratum on page 116.'

'I'm afraid not – at the moment.'

'How about a *Chevalier Audubon* 1840 – the full set, of course?'

'Er – not at the moment,' she said harshly. Her smile was now hanging by its teeth and eyebrows and wondering what it would hit when it dropped.

'You *do* sell books?' I said in my polite falsetto.

She looked me over. No smile now. Eyes medium to hard. Pose very straight and stiff. She waved silver fingernails at the glassed-in shelves. 'What do they look like – grapefruit?' she inquired tartly.

'Oh, that sort of thing hardly interests me, you know. Probably has duplicate sets of steel engravings, tuppence coloured and a penny plain. The usual vulgarity. No. I'm sorry. No.'

'I see.' She tried to jack the smile back upon her face. She was as sore as an alderman with the mumps. 'Perhaps Mr Geiger – but he's not in at the moment.' Her eyes studied me carefully. She knew as much about rare books as I knew about handling a flea circus.

'He might be in later?'

'I'm afraid not until late.'

'Too bad,' I said. 'Ah, too bad. I'll sit down and smoke a cigarette in one of these charming chairs. I have rather a blank afternoon. Nothing to think about but my trigonometry lesson.'

'Yes,' she said. 'Ye-es, of course.'

I stretched out in one and lit a cigarette with the round nickel lighter on the smoking stand. She still stood, holding her lower lip with her teeth, her eyes vaguely troubled. She nodded at last, turned slowly and walked back to her little desk in the corner. From behind the lamp she stared at me. I crossed my ankles and yawned. Her silver nails went out to the cradle phone on the desk, didn't touch it, dropped and began to tap on the desk.

Silence for about five minutes. The door opened and a tall hungry-looking bird with a cane and a big nose came in neatly, shut the door behind him against the pressure of the door closer, marched over to the desk and placed a wrapped parcel on the desk. He took a pin-seal wallet with gold corners from his pocket and showed the blonde something. She pressed a button on the desk. The tall bird went to the door in the panelled partition and opened it barely enough to slip through.

I finished my cigarette and lit another. The minutes dragged by. Horns tooted and grunted on the boulevard. A big red interurban car grumbled past. A traffic light gonged. The blonde leaned on her elbow and cupped a hand over her eyes and stared at me behind it. The partition door opened and the tall bird with the cane slid out. He had another wrapped parcel, the shape of a large book. He went over to the desk and paid money. He left as he had come, walking on the balls of his feet, breathing with his mouth open, giving me a sharp side glance as he passed.

I got to my feet, tipped my hat to the blonde and went out after him. He walked west, swinging his cane in a small tight arc just above his right shoe. He was easy to follow. His coat was cut from a rather loud piece of horse robe with shoulders so wide that his neck stuck up out of it like a celery stalk and his head wobbled on it as he walked. We went a block and a half. At the Highland Avenue traffic signal I pulled up beside him and let him see me. He gave me a casual, then a suddenly sharpened side glance, and quickly turned away. We crossed Highland with the green light and made another block. He stretched his long legs and had twenty yards on me at the corner. He turned right. A hundred feet up the hill he stopped and hooked his cane over his arm and fumbled a leather cigarette-case out of an inner pocket. He put a cigarette in his mouth, dropped his match, looked back when he picked it up, saw me watching him from the corner, and straightened up as if somebody had booted him from behind. He almost raised dust going up the block, walking with long gawky strides and jabbing his cane into the pavement. He turned left again. He had at least half a block on me when I reached the place where he had turned. He had me wheezing. This was a narrow tree-lined street with a retaining wall on one side and three bungalow courts on the other.

He was gone. I loafed along the block peering this way and that. At the second bungalow court I saw something. It was called The La Baba, a quiet dim place with a double row of tree-shaded bungalows. The central walk was lined with Italian cypresses trimmed short and chunky, something the shape of the oil jars in *Ali Baba and the Forty Thieves*. Behind the third jar a loud-patterned sleeve edge moved.

I leaned against a pepper tree in the parkway and waited. The thunder in the foothills was rumbling again. The glare of lightning was reflected on piled-up black clouds off to the south. A few tentative raindrops splashed down on the pavement and made spots as large as nickels.

The air was as still as the air in General Sternwood's orchid house.

The sleeve behind the tree showed again, then a big nose and one eye and some sandy hair without a hat on it. The eye stared at me. It disappeared. Its mate reappeared like a woodpecker on the other side of the tree. Five minutes went by. It got him. His type are half nerves. I heard a match strike and then whistling started. Then a dim shadow slipped along the grass to the next tree. Then he was out on the walk coming straight towards me, swinging the cane and whistling. A sour whistle with jitters in it. I stared vaguely up at the dark sky. He passed within ten feet of me and didn't give me a glance. He was safe now. He had ditched it.

I watched him out of sight and went up the central walk of The La Baba and parted the branches of the third cypress. I drew out a wrapped book and put it under my arm and went away from there. Nobody yelled at me.

5

Back on the boulevard I went into a drugstore phone booth and looked up Mr Arthur Gwynn Geiger's residence. He lived on Laverne Terrace, a hillside street off Laurel Canyon Boulevard. I dropped my nickel and dialled his number just for fun. Nobody answered. I turned to the classified section and noted a couple of bookstores within blocks of where I was.

The first I came to was on the north side, a large lower floor devoted to stationery and office supplies, a mass of books on the mezzanine. It didn't look the right place. I crossed the street and walked two blocks east to the other one. This was more like it, a narrowed cluttered little shop stacked with books from floor to ceiling and four or five browsers taking their time putting thumb marks on the new jackets. Nobody paid any attention to them. I shoved on back into the store, passed through a partition and found a small dark woman reading a law book at a desk.

I flipped my wallet open on her desk and let her look at the buzzer pinned to the flap. She looked at it, took her glasses off and leaned back in her chair. I put the wallet away. She had the fine-drawn face of an intelligent Jewess. She stared at me and said nothing.

I said: 'Would you do me a favour, a very small favour?'

'I don't know. What is it?' She had a smoothly husky voice.

'You know Geiger's store across the street, two blocks west?'

'I think I may have passed it.'

'It's a bookstore,' I said. 'Not your kind of bookstore. You know darn well.'

She curled her lips slightly and said nothing. 'You know Geiger by sight?' I asked.

'I'm sorry. I don't know Mr Geiger.'

'Then you couldn't tell me what he looks like?'

Her lip curled some more. 'Why should I?'

'No reason at all. If you don't want to, I can't make you.'

She looked out through the partition door and leaned back again. 'That was a sheriff's star, wasn't it?'

'Honorary deputy. Doesn't mean a thing. It's worth a dime cigar.'

'I see.' She reached for a pack of cigarettes and shook one loose and reached for it with her lips. I held a match for her. She thanked me, leaned back again and regarded me through smoke. She said carefully:

'You wish to know what he looks like and you don't want to interview him?'

'He's not there,' I said.

'I presume he will be. After all, it's his store.'

'I don't want to interview him just yet,' I said.

She looked out through the open doorway again. I said: 'Know anything about rare books?'

'You could try me.'

'Would you have a *Ben Hur*, 1860, third edition, the one with the duplicated line on page 116?'

She pushed her yellow law book to one side and reached a fat volume up on the desk, leafed it through, found her page, and studied it. 'Nobody would,' she said without looking up. 'There isn't one.'

'Right.'

'What in the world are you driving at?'

'The girl in Geiger's store didn't know that.'

She looked up. 'I see. You interest me. Rather vaguely.'

'I'm a private dick on a case. Perhaps I ask too much. It didn't seem much to me somehow.'

She blew a soft grey smoke ring and poked her finger through. It came to pieces in frail wisps. She spoke smoothly, indifferently. 'In his early forties, I should judge. Medium height, fattish. Would weigh about a hundred and sixty pounds. Fat face, Charlie Chan moustache, thick soft neck. Soft all over. Well dressed, goes without a hat, affects a knowledge of antiques and hasn't any. Oh yes. His left eye is glass.'

'You'd make a good cop,' I said.

She put the reference book back on an open shelf at the end of her desk, and opened the law book in front of her again. 'I hope not,' she said. She put her glasses on.

I thanked her and left. The rain had started. I ran for it, with the wrapped book under my arm. My car was on a side street pointing at the boulevard almost opposite

Geiger's store. I was well sprinkled before I got there. I tumbled into the car and ran both windows up and wiped my parcel off with my handkerchief. Then I opened it up.

I knew about what it would be, of course. A heavy book, well bound, handsomely printed in handset type on fine paper. Larded with full-page arty photographs. Photos and letter-press were alike of an indescribable filth. The book was not new. Dates were stamped on the front endpaper, in and out dates. A rent book. A lending library of elaborate smut.

I re-wrapped the book and locked it up behind the seat. A racket like that, out in the open on the boulevard, seemed to mean plenty of protection. I sat there and poisoned myself with cigarette smoke and listened to the rain and thought about it.

6

Rain filled the gutters and splashed knee-high off the pavement. Big cops in slickers that shone like gun barrels had a lot of fun carrying giggling girls across the bad places. The rain drummed hard on the roof of the car and the burbank top began to leak. A pool of water formed on the floorboards for me to keep my feet in. It was too early in the fall for that kind of rain. I struggled into a trench coat and made a dash for the nearest drugstore and bought myself a pint of whisky. Back in the car I used enough of it to keep warm and interested. I was long overparked, but the cops were too busy carrying girls and blowing whistles to bother about that.

In spite of the rain, or perhaps even because of it, there was business done at Geiger's. Very nice cars stopped in front and very nice-looking people went in and out with wrapped parcels. They were not all men.

He showed about four o'clock. A cream-coloured coupé stopped in front of the store and I caught a glimpse of the fat face and the Charlie Chan moustache as he dodged out of it and into the store. He was hatless and wore a belted green leather raincoat. I couldn't see his glass eye at that distance. A tall and very good-looking kid in a jerkin came out of the store and rode the coupé off around the corner and came back walking, his glistening black hair plastered with rain.

Another hour went by. It got dark and the rain-clouded lights of the stores were soaked up by the black street. Street-car bells jangled crossly. At around five-fifteen the tall boy in the jerkin came out of Geiger's with an umbrella and went after the cream-coloured coupé. When he had it in front Geiger came out and the tall boy held the umbrella over Geiger's bare head. He folded it, shook it off and handed it into the car. He dashed back into the store. I started my motor.

The coupé went west on the boulevard, which forced me to make a left turn and a lot of enemies, including a motorman who stuck his head out into the rain to bawl me out. I was two blocks behind the coupé before I got in the groove. I hoped Geiger was on his way home. I caught sight of him two or three times and then made him turning north into Laurel Canyon Drive. Half-way up the grade he turned left and took a curving ribbon of wet concrete which was called Laverne Terrace. It was a narrow street with a high bank on one side and a scattering of cabin-like houses built down the slope on the other side, so that their roofs were not very much above road level. Their front windows were masked by hedges and shrubs. Sodden trees dripped all over the landscape.

Geiger had his lights on and I hadn't. I speeded up and passed him on a curve, picked a number off a house as I went by and turned at the end of the block. He had already stopped. His car lights were tilted in at the garage of a small house with a square box hedge so arranged that it masked the front door completely. I watched him come out of the garage with his umbrella up and go in through the hedge. He didn't act as if he expected anybody to be tailing him. Light went on in the house. I drifted down to the next house above it, which seemed empty but had no signs out. I parked, aired out the convertible, had a drink from my bottle, and sat. I didn't know what I was waiting for, but something told me to wait. Another army of sluggish minutes dragged by.

Two cars came up the hill and went over the crest. It seemed to be a very quiet street. At a little after six more bright lights bobbed through the driving rain. It was pitch-black by then. A car dragged to a stop in front of Geiger's house. The filaments of its lights glowed dimly and died. The door opened and a woman got out. A small slim woman in a vagabond hat and a transparent raincoat. She went in through the box maze. A bell rang faintly, light through the rain, a closing door, silence.

I reached a flash out of my car pocket and went downgrade and looked at the car. It was a Packard convertible, maroon or dark brown. The left window was down. I felt for the licence holder and poked light at it. The registration read: Carmen Sternwood, 3765 Alta Brea Crescent, West Hollywood. I went back to my car again and sat and sat. The top dripped on my knees and my stomach burned from the whisky. No more cars came up the hill. No lights went on in the house before which I was parked. It seemed like a nice neighbourhood to have bad habits in.

At seven-twenty a single flash of hard white light shot out of Geiger's house like a wave of summer lightning. As the darkness folded back on it and ate it up a thin tinkling scream echoed out and lost itself among the rain-drenched trees. I was out of the car and on my way before the echoes died.

There was no fear in the scream. It had a sound of half-pleasurable shock, an accent of drunkenness, an overtone of pure idiocy. It was a nasty sound. It made me think of men in white and barred windows and hard narrow cots with leather wrist and ankle straps fastened to them. The Geiger hideaway was perfectly silent again when I hit the gap in the hedge and dodged around the angle that masked the front door. There was an iron ring in a lion's mouth for a knocker. I reached for it, I had hold of it. At that exact instant, as if somebody had been waiting for the cue, three shots boomed in the house. There was a sound that might have been a long harsh sigh. Then a soft messy thump. And then rapid footsteps in the house – going away.

The door fronted on a narrow run, like a footbridge over a gully, that filled the gap between the house wall and the edge of the bank. There was no porch, no solid ground, no way to get around to the back. The back entrance was at the top of a flight of wooden steps that rose from the alley-like street below. I knew this because I heard a clatter of feet on the steps, going down. Then I heard the sudden roar of a starting car. It faded swiftly into the distance. I thought the sound was echoed by another car, but I wasn't sure. The house in front of me was as silent as a vault. There wasn't any hurry. What was in there was in there.

I straddled the fence at the side of the runway and leaned far out to the draped but unscreened French window and tried to look in at the crack where the drapes came together. I saw lamplight on a wall and one end of a bookcase. I got back on the runway and took all of it and some of the hedge and gave the front door the heavy shoulder. This was foolish. About the only part of a California house you can't put your foot through is the front door. All it did was hurt my shoulder and make me mad. I climbed over the railing again and kicked the French window in, used my hat for a glove and pulled out most of the lower small pane of glass. I could now reach in and draw a bolt that fastened the window to the sill. The rest was easy. There was no top bolt. The catch gave. I climbed in and pulled the drapes off my face.

Neither of the two people in the room paid any attention to the way I came in, although only one of them was dead.

7

It was a wide room, the whole width of the house. It had a low beamed ceiling and brown plaster walls decked out with strips of Chinese embroidery, and Chinese and Japanese prints in grained wood frames. There were low bookshelves, there was a thick pinkish Chinese rug in which a gopher could have spent a week without showing his nose above the nap. There were floor cushions, bits of odd silk tossed around, as if whoever lived there had to have a piece he could reach out and thumb. There was a broad low divan of old rose tapestry. It had a wad of clothes on it, including lilac-coloured silk underwear. There was a big carved lamp on a pedestal, two other standing lamps with jade-green shades and long tassels. There was a black desk with carved gargoyles at the corners and behind it a yellow satin cushion on a polished black chair with carved arms and back. The room contained an odd assortment of odours, of which the most emphatic at the moment seemed to be the pungent aftermath of cordite and the sickish aroma of ether.

On a sort of low dais at one end of the room there was a high-backed teakwood chair in which Miss Carmen

Sternwood was sitting on a fringed orange shawl. She was sitting very straight, with her hands on the arms of the chair, her knees close together, her body stiffly erect in the pose of an Egyptian goddess, her chin level, her small bright teeth shining between her parted lips. Her eyes were wide open. The dark slate colour of the iris had devoured the pupil. They were mad eyes. She seemed to be unconscious, but she didn't have the pose of unconsciousness. She looked as if, in her mind, she was doing something very important and making a fine job of it. Out of her mouth came a tinny chuckling noise which didn't change her expression or even move her lips.

She was wearing a pair of long jade earrings. They were nice earrings and had probably cost a couple of hundred dollars. She wasn't wearing anything else.

She had a beautiful body, small, lithe, compact, firm, rounded. Her skin in the lamplight had the shimmering lustre of a pearl. Her legs didn't quite have the raffish grace of Mrs Regan's legs, but they were very nice. I looked her over without either embarrassment or ruttishness. As a naked girl she was not there in that room at all. She was just a dope. To me she was always just a dope.

I stopped looking at her, and looked at Geiger. He was on his back on the floor, beyond the fringe of the Chinese rug, in front of a thing that looked like a totem pole. It had a profile like an eagle and its wide round eye was a camera lens. The lens was aimed at the naked girl in the chair. There was a blackened flash bulb clipped to the side of the totem pole. Geiger was wearing Chinese slippers with thick felt soles, and his legs were in black satin pyjamas and the upper part of him wore a Chinese embroidered coat, the front of which was mostly blood. His glass eye shone brightly up at me and was by far the most lifelike thing about him. At a glance none of the three shots I heard had missed. He was very dead.

The flash bulb was the sheet lightning I had seen. The crazy scream was the doped and naked girl's reaction to it. The three shots had been somebody else's idea of how the proceedings might be given a new twist. The idea of the lad who had gone down the back steps and slammed into a car and raced away. I could see merit in his point of view.

A couple of fragile gold-veined glasses rested on a red lacquer tray on the end of the black desk, beside a pot-bellied flagon of brown liquid. I took the stopper out and sniffed at it. It smelled of ether and something else, possibly laudanum. I had never tried the mixture but it seemed to go pretty well with the Geiger *ménage*.

I listened to the rain hitting the roof and the north windows. Beyond was no other sound, no cars, no siren, just the rain beating. I went over to the divan and peeled off my trench coat and pawed through the girl's clothes. There was a pale green rough wool dress of the pull-on type, with half sleeves. I thought I might be able to handle it. I decided to pass up her underclothes, not from feelings of delicacy, but because I couldn't see myself putting her pants on and snapping her brassière. I took the dress over to the teak chair on the dais. Miss Sternwood smelled of ether also, at a distance of several feet. The tinny chuckling noise was still coming from her and a little froth oozed down her chin. I slapped her face. She blinked and stopped chuckling. I slapped her again.

'Come on,' I said brightly. 'Let's be nice. Let's get dressed.'

She peered at me, her slaty eyes as empty as holes in a mask. 'Gugugoterell,' she said.

I slapped her around a little more. She didn't mind the slaps. They didn't bring her out of it. I set to work with the dress. She didn't mind that either. She let me hold her arms up and she spread her fingers out wide, as if that was cute. I got her hands through the sleeves, pulled the dress down over her back, and stood her up. She fell into my arms giggling. I set her back in the chair and got her stockings and shoes on her.

'Let's take a little walk,' I said. 'Let's take a nice little walk.'

We took a little walk. Part of the time her earrings banged against my chest and part of the time we did the splits in unison, like adagio dancers. We walked over to Geiger's body and back. I had her look at him. She thought he was cute. She giggled and tried to tell me so, but she just bubbled. I walked her over to the divan and spread her out on it. She hiccuped twice, giggled a little and went to sleep. I stuffed her belongings into my pockets and went over behind the totem pole thing. The camera was there all right, set inside it, but there was no plate-holder in the camera. I looked around on the floor, thinking he might have got it out before he was shot. No plateholder. I took hold of his limp chilling hand and rolled him a little. No plateholder. I didn't like this development.

I went into a hall at the back of the room and investigated the house. There was a bathroom on the right and a locked door, a kitchen at the back. The kitchen window had been jimmied. The screen was gone and the place where the hook had pulled out showed on the sill. The back door was unlocked. I left it unlocked and looked into a bedroom on the left side of the hall. It was neat, fussy, womanish. The bed had a flounced cover. There was perfume on the triple-mirrored dressing-table, beside a handkerchief, some loose money, a man's brushes, a keyholder. A man's clothes were in the closet and a man's slippers under the flounced edge of the bed cover. Mr Geiger's room. I took the keyholder back to the living-room and went through the desk. There was a locked steel box in the deep drawer. I used one of the keys on it. There was nothing in it but a blue leather book with an index and a lot of writing in code, in the same slanting printing that had written to General Sternwood. I put the notebook in my pocket, wiped the steel box where I had touched it, locked the desk up, pocketed the keys, turned the gas logs off in the fireplace, wrapped myself in my coat and tried to rouse Miss Sternwood. It couldn't be done. I crammed her vagabond hat on her head and swathed her in her coat and carried her out to her car. I went back and put all the lights out and shut the front door, dug her keys out of her bag and started the Packard. We went off down the hill without lights. It was less than ten minutes' drive to Alta Brea Crescent. Carmen spent them snoring and breathing ether in my face. I couldn't keep her head off my shoulder. It was all I could do to keep it out of my lap.

8

There was dim light behind narrow leaded panes in the side door of the Sternwood mansion. I stopped the Packard under the *porte-cochère* and emptied my pockets out on the seat. The girl snored in the corner, her hat tilted rakishly over her nose, her hands hanging limp in the folds of the raincoat. I got out and rang the bell. Steps came slowly, as if from a long dreary distance. The door opened and the straight, silvery butler looked out at me. The light from the hall made a halo of his hair.

He said: 'Good evening, sir' politely and looked past me at the Packard. His eyes came back to look at my eyes.

'Is Mrs Regan in?'

'No, sir.'

'The General is asleep, I hope?'

'Yes. The evening is his best time for sleeping.'

'How about Mrs Regan's maid?'

'Mathilda? She's here, sir.'

'Better get her down here. The job needs the woman's touch. Take a look in the car and you'll see why.'

He took a look in the car. He came back. 'I see,' he said. 'I'll get Mathilda.'

‘Mathilda will do right by her,’ I said.

‘We all try to do right by her,’ he said.

‘I guess you’ll have had practice,’ I said.

He let that one go. ‘Well, good night,’ I said. ‘I’m leaving it in your hands.’

‘Very good, sir. May I call you a cab?’

‘Positively not,’ I said. ‘As a matter of fact I’m not here. You’re just seeing things.’

He smiled then. He gave me a duck of his head and I turned and walked down the driveway and out of the gates.

Ten blocks of that, winding down curved rainswept streets, under the steady drip of trees, past lighted windows in big houses in ghostly enormous grounds, vague clusters of eaves and gables and lighted windows high on the hillside, remote and inaccessible, like witch houses in a forest. I came out at a service station glaring with wasted light, where a bored attendant in a white cap and a dark blue windbreaker sat hunched on a stool, inside the steamed glass, reading a paper. I started in, then kept going. I was as wet as I could get already. And on a night like that you can grow a beard waiting for a taxi. And taxi drivers remember.

I made it back to Geiger’s house in something over half an hour of nimble walking. There was nobody there, no car on the street except my own car in front of the next house. It looked as dismal as a lost dog. I dug my bottle of rye out of it and poured half of what was left down my throat and got inside to light a cigarette. I smoked half of it, threw it away, got out again and went down to Geiger’s. I unlocked the door and stepped into the still warm darkness and stood there, dripping quietly on the floor and listening to the rain. I groped to a lamp and lit it.

The first thing I noticed was that a couple of strips of embroidered silk were gone from the wall. I hadn't counted them, but the spaces of brown plaster stood out naked and obvious. I went a little farther and put another lamp on. I looked at the totem pole. At its foot, beyond the margin of the Chinese rug, on the bare floor another rug had been spread. It hadn't been there before. Geiger's body had. Geiger's body was gone.

That froze me. I pulled my lips back against my teeth and leered at the glass eye in the totem pole. I went through the house again. Everything was exactly as it had been. Geiger wasn't in his flounced bed or under it or in his closet. He wasn't in the kitchen or the bathroom. That left the locked door on the right of the hall. One of Geiger's keys fitted the lock. The room inside was interesting, but Geiger wasn't in it. It was interesting because it was so different from Geiger's room. It was a hard bare masculine bedroom with a polished wood floor, a couple of small throw rugs in an Indian design, two straight chairs, a bureau in dark grained wood with a man's toilet set and two black candles in foot-high brass candlesticks. The bed was narrow and looked hard and had a maroon batik cover. The room felt cold. I locked it up again, wiped the knob off with my handkerchief, and went back to the totem pole. I knelt down and squinted along the nap of the rug to the front door. I thought I could see two parallel grooves pointing that way, as though heels had dragged. Whoever had done it had meant business. Dead men are heavier than broken hearts.

It wasn't the law. They would have been there still, just about getting warmed up with their pieces of string and chalk and their cameras and dusting powders and their nickel cigars. They would have been very much there. It wasn't the killer. He had left too fast. He must have seen the girl. He couldn't be sure she was too batty to see him. He would be on his way to distant places. I couldn't guess the answer, but it was all right with me if somebody wanted Geiger missing instead of just murdered. It gave me a chance to find out if I could tell it leaving Carmen Sternwood out. I locked up again, choked my car to life and rode off home to a shower, dry clothes and a late dinner. After that I sat around in the apartment and drank too much hot toddy trying to crack the code in Geiger's blue indexed notebook. All I could be sure of was that it was a list of names and addresses probably of the customers. There were over four hundred of them. That made it a nice racket, not to mention any blackmail angles, and there were probably plenty of those. Any name on the list might be a prospect as the killer. I didn't envy the police their job when it was handed to them.

I went to bed full of whisky and frustration and dreamed about a man in a bloody Chinese coat who chased a naked girl with long jade earrings while I ran after them and tried to take a photograph with an empty camera.

9

The next morning was bright, clear and sunny. I woke up with a motorman's glove in my mouth, drank two cups of coffee and went through the morning papers. I didn't find any reference to Mr Arthur Gwynn Geiger in either of them. I was shaking the wrinkles out of my damp suit when the phone rang. It was Bernie Ohls, the DA's chief investigator, who had given me the lead to General Sternwood.

'Well, how's the boy?' he began. He sounded like a man who had slept well and didn't owe too much money.

'I've got a hangover,' I said.

'Tsk, tsk.' He laughed absently and then his voice became a shade too casual, a cagey cop voice. 'Seen General Sternwood yet?'

'Uh-huh.'

'Done anything for him?'

'Too much rain,' I answered, if that was an answer.

'They seem to be a family things happen to. A big Buick belonging to one of them is washing about in the surf off Lido fish pier.'

I held the telephone tight enough to crack it. I also held my breath.

'Yeah,' Ohls said cheerfully. 'A nice new Buick sedan all messed up with sand and sea water . . . Oh, I almost forgot. There's a guy inside it.'

I let my breath out so slowly that it hung on my lips. 'Regan?' I asked.

'Huh? Who? Oh, you mean the ex-legger the eldest girl picked up and went and married. I never saw him. What would he be doing down there?'

'Quit stalling. What would anybody be doing down there?'

'I don't know, pal. I'm dropping down to look-see. Want to go along?'

'Yes.'

'Snap it up,' he said. 'I'll be in my hutch.'

Shaved, dressed and lightly breakfasted I was at the Hall of Justice in less than an hour. I rode up to the seventh floor and went along to the group of small offices used by the DA's men. Ohls's was no larger than the others, but he had it to himself. There was nothing on his desk but a blotter, a cheap pen set, his hat and one of his feet. He was a medium-sized blondish man with stiff white eyebrows, calm eyes and well-kept teeth. He looked like anybody you would pass on the street. I happened to know he had killed nine men – three of them when he was covered, or somebody thought he was.

He stood up and pocketed a flat tin of toy cigars called Entractes, jiggled the one in his mouth up and down and looked at me carefully along his nose, with his head thrown back.

'It's not Regan,' he said. 'I checked. Regan's a big guy, as tall as you and a shade heavier. This is a young kid.'

I didn't say anything.

'What made Regan skip out?' Ohls asked. 'You interested in that?'

'I don't think so,' I said.

'When a guy out of the liquor traffic marries into a rich family and then waves good-bye to a pretty dame and a couple million legitimate bucks – that's enough to make even me think. I guess you thought that was a secret.'

'Uh-huh.'

'Okey, keep buttoned, kid. No hard feelings.' He came around the desk tapping his pockets and reaching for his hat.

'I'm not looking for Regan,' I said.

He fixed the lock on his door and we went down to the official parking lot and got into a small blue sedan. We drove out Sunset, using the siren once in a while to beat a signal. It was a crisp morning, with just enough snap in the air to make life seem simple and sweet, if you didn't have too much on your mind. I had.

It was thirty miles to Lido on the coast highway, the first ten of them through traffic. Ohls made the run in three-quarters of an hour. At the end of that time we skidded to a stop in front of a faded stucco arch and I took my feet out of the floorboards and we got out. A long pier railed with white two-by-fours stretched seaward from the arch. A knot of people leaned out at the far end and a motor-cycle officer stood under the arch keeping another group of people from going out on the pier. Cars were parked on both sides of the highway, the usual ghouls, of both sexes. Ohls showed the motor-cycle officer his badge and we went out on the pier, into a loud fish smell which one night's hard rain hadn't even dented.

'There she is – on the power barge,' Ohls said, pointing with one of his toy cigars.

A low black barge with a wheelhouse like a tug's was crouched against the pilings at the end of the pier. Something that glistened in the morning sunlight was on its deck, with hoist chains still around it, a large black and chromium car. The arm of the hoist had been swung back into position and lowered to deck level. Men stood around the car. We went down slippery steps to the deck.

Ohls said hello to a deputy in green khaki and a man in plain clothes. The barge crew of three men leaned against the front of the wheelhouse and chewed tobacco. One of them was rubbing at his wet hair with a dirty bath-towel. That would be the man who had gone down into the water to put the chains on.

We looked the car over. The front bumper was bent, one headlight smashed, the other bent up but the glass still unbroken. The radiator shell had a big dent in it, and the paint and nickel were scratched up all over the car. The upholstery was sodden and black. None of the tyres seemed to be damaged.

The driver was still draped around the steering post with his head at an unnatural angle to his shoulders. He was a slim dark-haired kid who had been good-looking not so long ago. Now his face was bluish white and his eyes were a faint dull gleam under the lowered lids and his open mouth had sand in it. On the left side of his forehead there was a dull bruise that stood out against the whiteness of the skin.

Ohls backed away, made a noise in his throat and put a match to his little cigar. 'What's the story?'

The uniformed man pointed up at the rubbernecks on the end of the pier. One of them was fingering a place where the white two-by-fours had been broken through in a wide space. The splintered wood showed yellow and clean, like fresh-cut pine.

'Went through there. Must have hit pretty hard. The rain stopped early down here, around nine p.m. The broken wood's dry inside. That puts it after the rain stopped. She fell in plenty of water not to be banged up worse, not more than half tide or she'd have drifted farther, and not more than half tide going out or she'd have crowded the piles. That makes it around ten last night. Maybe nine-thirty, not earlier. She shows under the water when the boys come down to fish this morning, so we get the barge to hoist her out and we find the dead guy.'

The plain-clothes man scuffed at the deck with the toe of his shoe. Ohls looked sideways along his eyes at me, and twitched his little cigar like a cigarette.

'Drunk?' he asked, of nobody in particular.

The man who had been towelling his head went over to the rail and cleared his throat in a loud hawk that made everyone look at him. 'Got some sand,' he said, and spat. 'Not as much as the boy friend got – but some.'

The uniformed man said: 'Could have been drunk. Showing off all alone in the rain. Drunks will do anything.'

'Drunk, hell,' the plain-clothes man said. 'The hand throttle's set half-way down and the guy's been sapped on the side of the head. Ask me and I'll call it murder.'

Ohls looked at the man with the towel. 'What do you think, buddy?'

The man with the towel looked flattered. He grinned. 'I say suicide, Mac. None of my business, but you ask me, I say suicide. First off the guy ploughed an awful straight furrow down that pier. You can read his tread marks all the way nearly. That puts it after the rain like the Sheriff said. Then he hit the pier hard and clean or he don't go through and land right side up. More likely turned over a couple of times. So he had plenty of speed and hit the rail square. That's more than half-throttle. He could have done that with his hand falling and he could have hurt his head falling too.'

Ohls said: 'You got eyes, buddy. Frisked him?' he asked the deputy. The deputy looked at me, then at the crew against the wheelhouse. 'Okey, save that,' Ohls said.

A small man with glasses and a tired face and a black bag came down the steps from the pier. He picked out a fairly clean spot on the deck and put the bag down. Then he took his hat off and rubbed the back of his neck and stared out to sea, as if he didn't know where he was or what he had come for.

Ohls said: 'There's your customer, Doc. Dived off the pier last night. Around nine to ten. That's all we know.'

The small man looked in at the dead man morosely. He fingered the head, peered at the bruise on the temple, moved the head around with both hands, felt the man's ribs. He lifted a lax dead hand and stared at the fingernails. He let it fall and watched it fall. He stepped back and opened his bag and took out a printed pad of D.O.A. forms and began to write over a carbon.

'Broken neck's the apparent cause of death,' he said, writing. 'Which means there won't be much water in him. Which means he's due to start getting stiff pretty quick now he's out in the air. Better get him out of the car before he does. You won't like doing it after.'

Ohls nodded. 'How long dead, Doc?'

'I wouldn't know.'

Ohls looked at him sharply and took the little cigar out of his mouth and looked at that sharply. 'Pleased to know you, Doc. A coroner's man that can't guess within five minutes has me beat.'

The little man grinned sourly and put his pad in his bag and clipped his pencil back on his waistcoat. 'If he ate dinner last night, I'll tell you – if I know what time he ate it. But not within five minutes.'

'How would he get that bruise – falling?'

The little man looked at the bruise again. 'I don't think so. That blow came from something covered. And it had already bled subcutaneously while he was alive.'

'Blackjack, huh?'

'Very likely.'

The little M.E.'s man nodded, picked his bag off the deck and went back up the steps to the pier. An ambulance was backing into position outside the stucco arch. Ohls looked at me and said: 'Let's go. Hardly worth the ride, was it?'

We went back along the pier and got into Ohls's sedan again. He wrestled it around on the highway and drove back towards town along a three-lane highway washed clean by the rain, past low rolling hills of yellow-white sand terraced with pink moss. Seaward a few gulls wheeled and swooped over something in the surf and far out a white yacht looked as if it was hanging in the sky.

Ohls cocked his chin at me and said: 'Know him?'

'Sure. The Sternwood chauffeur. I saw him dusting that very car out there yesterday.'

'I don't want to crowd you, Marlowe. Just tell me, did the job have anything to do with him?'

'No. I don't even know his name.'

'Owen Taylor. How do I know? Funny about that. About a year or so back we had him in the cooler on a Mann Act rap. It seems he run Sternwood's hotcha daughter, the young one, off to Yuma. The sister ran after them and brought them back and had Owen heaved into the icebox. Then next day she comes down to the D.A. and gets him to beg the kid off with the U.S. 'cutor. She says the kid meant to marry her sister and wanted to, only the sister can't see it. All *she* wanted was to kick a few high ones off the bar and have herself a party. So we let the kid go and then darned if they don't have him come back to work. And a little later we get the routine report on his prints from Washington, and he's got a prior back in Indiana, attempted hold-up six years ago. He got off with a six months in the county jail, the very one Dillinger bust out of. We hand that to the Sternwoods and they keep him on just the same. What do you think of that?'

'They seem to be a screwy family,' I said. 'Do they know about last night?'

‘No. I gotta go up against them now.’

‘Leave the old man out of it, if you can.’

‘Why?’

‘He has enough troubles and he’s sick.’

‘You mean Regan?’

I scowled. ‘I don’t know anything about Regan, I told you. I’m not looking for Regan. Regan hasn’t bothered anybody that I know of.’

Ohls said: ‘Oh,’ and stared thoughtfully out to sea and the sedan nearly went off the road. For the rest of the drive back to town he hardly spoke. He dropped me off in Hollywood near the Chinese Theatre and turned back west to Alta Brea Crescent. I ate lunch at a counter and looked at an afternoon paper and couldn’t find anything about Geiger in it.

After lunch I walked east on the boulevard to have another look at Geiger’s store.

10

The lean black-eyed credit jeweller was standing in his entrance in the same position as the afternoon before. He gave me the same knowing look as I turned in. The store looked just the same. The same lamp glowed on the small desk in the corner and the same ash blonde in the same black suede-like dress got up from behind it and came towards me with the same tentative smile on her face.

'Was it –?' she said and stopped. Her silver nails twitched at her side. There was an overtone of strain in her smile. It wasn't a smile at all. It was a grimace. She just thought it was a smile.

'Back again,' I said airily, and waved a cigarette. 'Mr Geiger in to-day?'

'I'm – I'm afraid not. No – I'm afraid not. Let me see – you wanted –?'

I took my dark glasses off and tapped them delicately on the inside of my left wrist. If you can weigh a hundred and ninety pounds and look like a fairy, I was doing my best.

'That was just a stall about those first editions,' I whispered. 'I have to be careful. I've got something he'll want. Something he's wanted for a long time.'

The silver fingernails touched the blonde hair over one small jet-buttoned ear. 'Oh, a salesman,' she said. 'Well – you might come in to-morrow. I think he'll be here to-morrow.'

'Drop the veil,' I said. 'I'm in the business too.'

Her eyes narrowed until they were a faint greenish glitter, like a forest pool far back in the shadow of trees. Her fingers clawed at her palm. She stared at me and chopped off a breath.

'Is he sick? I could go up to the house,' I said impatiently. 'I haven't got forever.'

'You – a – you – a –' her throat jammed. I thought she was going to fall on her nose. Her whole body shivered and her face fell apart like a bride's pie crust. She put it together again slowly, as if lifting a great weight, by sheer will power. The smile came back, with a couple of corners badly bent.

'No,' she said. 'No. He's out of town. That – wouldn't be any use. Can't you – come in – to-morrow?'

I had my mouth open to say something when the partition door opened a foot. The tall dark handsome boy in the jerkin looked out, pale-faced and tight-lipped, saw me, shut the door quickly again, but not before I had seen on the floor behind him a lot of wooden boxes lined with newspapers and packed loosely with books. A man in very new overalls was fussing with them. Some of Geiger's stock was being moved out.

When the door shut I put my dark glasses on again and touched my hat. 'To-morrow, then. I'd like to give you a card but you know how it is.'

'Ye-es. I know how it is.' She shivered a little more and made a faint sucking noise between her bright lips. I went out of the store and west on the boulevard to the corner and north on the street to the alley which ran behind the stores. A small black truck with wire sides and no lettering on it was backed up to Geiger's place. The man in the very new overalls was just heaving a box up on the tailboard. I went back to the boulevard and along the block next to Geiger's and found a taxi standing at a fireplug. A fresh-faced kid was reading a horror magazine behind the wheel. I leaned in and showed him a dollar: 'Tail job?'

He looked me over. 'Cop?'

'Private.'

He grinned. 'My meat, Jack.' He tucked the magazine over his rear-view mirror and I got into the cab. We went around the block and pulled up across from Geiger's alley, beside another fireplug.

There were about a dozen boxes on the truck when the man in overalls closed the screened doors and hooked the tailboard up and got in behind the wheel.

'Take him,' I told my driver.

The man in overalls gunned his motor, shot a glance up and down the alley and ran away fast in the other direction. He turned left out of the alley. We did the same. I caught a glimpse of the truck turning east on Franklin and told my driver to close in a little. He didn't or couldn't do it. I saw the truck two blocks away when we got to Franklin. We had it in sight to Vine and across Vine and all the way to Western. We saw it twice after

Western. There was a lot of traffic and the fresh-faced kid tailed from too far back. I was telling him about that without mincing words when the truck, now far ahead, turned north again. The street at which it turned was called Brittany Place. When we got to Brittany Place the truck had vanished.

The fresh-faced kid made comforting sounds at me through the panel and we went up the hill at four miles an hour looking for the truck behind bushes. Two blocks up, Brittany Place swung to the east and met Randall Place in a tongue of land on which there was a white apartment house with its front on Randall Place and its basement garage opening on Brittany. We were going past that and the fresh-faced kid was telling me the truck couldn't be far away when I looked through the arched entrance of the garage and saw it back in the dimness with its rear doors open again.

We went around to the front of the apartment house and I got out. There was nobody in the lobby, no switchboard. A wooden desk was pushed back against the wall beside a panel of gilt mailboxes. I looked the names over. A man named Joseph Brody had Apartment 405. A man named Joe Brody had received five thousand dollars from General Sternwood to stop playing with Carmen and find some other little girl to play with. It could be the same Joe Brody. I felt like giving odds on it.

I went around an elbow of wall to the foot of tiled stairs and the shaft of the automatic elevator. The top of the elevator was level with the floor. There was a door beside the shaft lettered 'Garage'. I opened it and went down narrow steps to the basement. The automatic elevator was propped open and the man in new overalls was grunting hard as he stacked heavy boxes in it. I stood beside him and lit a cigarette and watched him. He didn't like my watching him.

After a while I said: 'Watch the weight, bud. She's only tested for half a ton. Where's the stuff going?'

'Brody, four-o-five,' he said. 'Manager?'

'Yeah. Looks like a nice lot of loot.'

He glared at me with pale white-rimmed eyes. 'Books,' he snarled. 'A hundred pounds a box, easy, and me with a seventy-five pound back.'

'Well, watch the weight,' I said.

He got into the elevator with six boxes and shut the doors. I went back up the steps to the lobby and out to the street and the cab took me down-town again to my office building. I gave the fresh-faced kid too much money and he gave me a dog-eared business card which for once I didn't drop into the majolica jar of sand beside the elevator bank.

I had a room and a half on the seventh floor at the back. The half-room was an office split in two to make reception-rooms. Mine had my name on it and nothing else, and that only on the reception-room. I always left this unlocked, in case I had a client, and the client cared to sit down and wait.

I had a client.

11

She wore brownish speckled tweeds, a mannish shirt and tie, hand-carved walking shoes. Her stockings were just as sheer as the day before, but she wasn't showing as much of her legs. Her black hair was glossy under a brown Robin Hood hat that might have cost fifty dollars and looked as if you could have made it with one hand out of a desk blotter.

'Well, you *do* get up,' she said, wrinkling her nose at the faded red settee, the two odd semi-easy chairs, the net curtains that needed laundering and the boy's size library table with the venerable magazines on it to give the place a professional touch. 'I was beginning to think perhaps you worked in bed, like Marcel Proust.'

'Who's he?' I put a cigarette in my mouth and stared at her. She looked a little pale and strained, but she looked like a girl who could function under a strain.

'A French writer, a connoisseur in degenerates. You wouldn't know him.'

'Tut, tut,' I said. 'Come into my boudoir.'

She stood up and said: 'We didn't get along very well yesterday. Perhaps I was rude.'

'We were both rude,' I said. I unlocked the communicating door and held it for her. We went into the rest of my suite, which contained a rust-red carpet, not very young, five green filing cases, three of them full of California climate, an advertising calendar showing the Quins rolling around on a sky-blue floor, in pink dresses, with seal-brown hair and sharp black eyes as large as mammoth prunes. There were three near-walnut chairs, the usual desk with the usual blotter, pen set, ashtray and telephone, and the usual squeaky swivel chair behind it.

'You don't put on much of a front,' she said, sitting down at the customer's side of the desk.

I went over to the mail slot and picked up six envelopes, two letters and four pieces of advertising matter. I hung my hat on the telephone and sat down.

'Neither do the Pinkertons,' I said. 'You can't make much money at this trade, if you're honest. If you have a front, you're making money – or expect to.'

'Oh – are you honest?' she asked and opened her bag. She picked a cigarette out of a French enamel case, lit it with a pocket lighter, dropped case and lighter back into the bag and left the bag open.

'Painfully.'

'How did you ever get into this slimy kind of business then?'

'How did you come to marry a bootlegger?'

'My God, let's not start quarrelling again. I've been trying to get you on the phone all morning. Here and at your apartment.'

'About Owen?'

Her face tightened sharply. Her voice was soft. 'Poor Owen,' she said. 'So you know about that.'

'A DA's man took me down to Lido. He thought I might know something about it. But he knew much more than I did. He knew Owen wanted to marry your sister – once.'

She puffed silently at her cigarette and considered me with steady black eyes. 'Perhaps it wouldn't have been a bad idea,' she said quietly. 'He was in love with her. We don't find much of that in our circle.'

'He had a police record.'

She shrugged. She said negligently: 'He didn't know the right people. That's all a police record means in this rotten crime-ridden country.'

'I wouldn't go that far.'

She peeled her right glove off and bit her index finger at the first joint, looking at me with steady eyes. 'I didn't come to see you about Owen. Do you feel yet that you can tell me what my father wanted to see you about?'

'Not without his permission.'

'Was it about Carmen?'

'I can't even say that.' I finished filling a pipe and put a match to it. She watched the smoke for a moment. Then her hand went into her open bag and came out with a thick white envelope. She tossed it across the desk.

'You'd better look at it anyway,' she said.

I picked it up. The address was typewritten to Mrs Vivian Regan, 3765 Alta Brea Crescent, West Hollywood. Delivery had been by messenger service and the office stamp showed 8.35 a.m. as the time out. I opened the envelope and drew out the shiny 4¼ by 3¼ photo that was all there was inside.

It was Carmen sitting in Geiger's high-backed teak-wood chair on the dais, in her earrings and her birthday suit. Her eyes looked even a little crazier than as I remembered them. The back of the photo was blank. I put it back in the envelope.

'How much do they want?' I asked.

'Five thousand – for the negative and the rest of the prints. The deal has to be closed to-night, or they give the stuff to some scandal sheet.'

'The demand came how?'

'A woman telephoned me, about half an hour after this thing was delivered.'

'There's nothing in the scandal sheet angle. Juries convict without leaving the box on that stuff nowadays. What else is there?'

'Does there have to be something else?'

'Yes.'

She stared at me, a little puzzled. 'There is. The woman said there was a police jam connected with it and I'd better lay it on the line fast, or I'd be talking to my little sister through a wire screen.'

'Better,' I said. 'What kind of jam?'

'I don't know.'

'Where is Carmen now?'

'She's at home. She was sick last night. She's still in bed, I think.'

'Did she go out last night?'

'No. I was out, but the servants say she wasn't. I was

down at Las Olindas, playing roulette at Eddie Mars's Cypress Club. I lost my shirt.'

'So you like roulette. You would.'

She crossed her legs and lit another cigarette. 'Yes. I like roulette. All the Sternwoods like losing games, like roulette and marrying men that walk out on them and riding steeplechases at fifty-eight years old and being rolled on by a jumper and crippled for life. The Sternwoods have money. All it has bought them is a rain cheque.'

'What was Owen doing last night with your car?'

'Nobody knows. He took it without permission. We always let him take a car on his night off, but last night wasn't his night off.' She made a wry mouth. 'Do you think – ?'

'He knew about this nude photograph? How would I be able to say? I don't rule him out. Can you get five thousand in cash right away?'

'Not unless I tell Dad – or borrow it. I could probably borrow it from Eddie Mars. He ought to be generous with me, Heaven knows.'

'Better try that. You may need it in a hurry.'

She leaned back and hung an arm over the back of the chair. 'How about telling the police?'

'It's a good idea. But you won't do it.'

'Won't I?'

'No. You have to protect your father and your sister. You don't know what the police might turn up. It might be something they couldn't sit on. Though they usually try in blackmail cases.'

'Can you do anything?'

'I think I can. But I can't tell you why or how.'

'I like you,' she said suddenly. 'You believe in miracles. Would you have a drink in the office?'

I unlocked my deep drawer and got out my office bottle and two pony glasses. I filled them and we drank. She snapped her bag shut and pushed her chair back.

'I'll get the five grand,' she said. 'I've been a good customer of Eddie Mars. There's another reason why he should be nice to me, which you may not know.' She gave me one of those smiles the lips have forgotten before they reach the eyes. 'Eddie's blonde wife is the lady Rusty ran away with.'

I didn't say anything. She stared tightly at me and added: 'That doesn't interest you?'

'It ought to make it easier to find him – if I was looking for him. You don't think he's in this mess, do you?'

She pushed her empty glass at me. 'Give me another drink. You're the hardest guy to get anything out of. You don't even move your ears.'

I filled the little glass. 'You've got all you wanted out of me – a pretty good idea I'm not looking for your husband.'

She put the drink down very quickly. It made her gasp – or gave her an opportunity to gasp. She let a breath out slowly.

'Rusty was no crook. If he had been, it wouldn't have been for nickels. He carried fifteen thousand dollars, in bills. He called it his mad money. He had it when I married him and he had it when he left me. No – Rusty's not in on any cheap blackmail racket.'

She reached for the envelope and stood up. 'I'll keep in touch with you,' I said. 'If you want to leave me a message, the phone girl at my apartment house will take care of it.'

We walked over to the door. Tapping the white envelope against her knuckles, she said: 'You still feel you can't tell me what Dad –'

'I'd have to see him first.'

She took the photo out and stood looking at it, just inside the door. 'She has a beautiful little body, hasn't she?'

'Uh-huh.'

She leaned a little towards me. 'You ought to see mine,' she said gravely.

'Can it be arranged?'

She laughed suddenly and sharply and went half-way through the door, then turned her head to say coolly: 'You're as cold-blooded a beast as I ever met, Marlowe. Or can I call you Phil?'

'Sure.'

'You can call me Vivian.'

'Thanks, Mrs Regan.'

'Oh, go to hell, Marlowe.' She went on out and didn't look back.

I let the door shut and stood with my hand on it, staring at the hand. My face felt a little hot. I went back to the desk and put the whisky away and rinsed out the two pony glasses and put them away.

I took my hat off the phone and called the DA's office, and asked for Bernie Ohls.

He was back in his cubby-hole. 'Well, I let the old man alone,' he said. 'The butler said he or one of the girls would tell him. This Owen Taylor lived over the garage and I went through his stuff. Parents at Dubuque, Iowa. I wired the Chief of Police there to find out what they want done. The Sternwood family will pay for it.'

'Suicide?' I asked.

'No can tell. He didn't leave any notes. He had no leave to take the car. Everybody was home last night but Mrs Regan. She was down at Las Olindas with a playboy named Larry Cobb. I checked on that. I know a lad on one of the tables.'

'You ought to stop some of that flash gambling,' I said.

'With the syndicate we got in this country? Be your age, Marlowe. That sap mark on the boy's head bothers me. Sure you can't help me on this?'

I liked his putting it that way. It let me say no without actually lying. We said good-bye and I left the office, bought all three afternoon papers and rode a taxi down to the Hall of Justice to get my car out of the lot. There was nothing in any of the papers about Geiger. I took another look at his blue notebook, but the code was just as stubborn as it had been the night before.

12

The trees on the upper side of Laverne Terrace had fresh green leaves after the rain. In the cool afternoon sunlight I could see the steep drop of the hill and the flight of steps down which the killer had run after his three shots in the darkness. Two small houses fronted on the street below. They might or might not have heard the shots.

There was no activity in front of Geiger's house or anywhere along the block. The box hedge looked green and peaceful and the shingles on the roof were still damp. I drove past slowly, gnawing at an idea. I hadn't looked in the garage the night before. Once Geiger's body slipped away I hadn't really wanted to find it. It would force my hand. But dragging him to the garage, to his own car and driving that off into one of the hundred-odd lonely canyons around Los Angeles would be a good way to dispose of him for days or even for weeks. That supposed two things: a key to his car and two in the party. It would narrow the sector of search quite a lot, especially as I had had his personal keys in my pocket when it happened.

I didn't get a chance to look at the garage. The doors were shut and padlocked and something moved behind the hedge as I drew level. A woman in a green and white check coat and a small button of a hat on soft blonde hair stepped out of the maze and stood looking wild-eyed at my car, as if she hadn't heard it come up the hill. Then she turned swiftly and dodged back out of sight. It was Carmen Sternwood, of course.

I went on up the street and parked and walked back. In the daylight it seemed an exposed and dangerous thing to do. I went in through the hedge. She stood there straight and silent against the locked front door. One hand went slowly up to her teeth and her teeth bit at her funny thumb. There were purple smears under her eyes and her face was gnawed white by nerves.

She half smiled at me. She said: 'Hello,' in a thin, brittle voice. 'What – what –?' That tailed off and she went back to the thumb.

'Remember me?' I said. 'Doghouse Reilly, the man that grew too tall. Remember?'

She nodded and a quick jerky smile played across her face.

'Let's go in,' I said. 'I've got a key. Swell, huh?'

'Wha– wha–?'

I pushed her to one side and put the key in the door and opened it and pushed her in through it. I shut the door again and stood there sniffing. The place was horrible by daylight. The Chinese junk on the walls, the rug, the fussy lamps, the teakwood stuff, the sticky riot of colours, the totem pole, the flagon of ether and laudanum – all this in the daytime had a stealthy nastiness, like a fag party.

The girl and I stood looking at each other. She tried to

keep a cute little smile on her face but her face was too tired to be bothered. It kept going blank on her. The smile would wash off like water off sand and her pale skin had a harsh granular texture under the stunned and stupid blankness of her eyes. A whitish tongue licked at the corners of her mouth. A pretty, spoiled and not very bright little girl who had gone very, very wrong, and nobody was doing anything about it. To hell with the rich. They made me sick. I rolled a cigarette in my fingers and pushed some books out of the way and sat on the end of the black desk. I lit my cigarette, puffed a plume of smoke and watched the thumb and tooth act for a while in silence. Carmen stood in front of me, like a bad girl in the principal's office.

'What are you doing here?' I asked her finally.

She picked at the cloth of her coat and didn't answer.

'How much do you remember of last night?'

She answered that – with a foxy glitter rising at the back of her eyes. 'Remember what? I was sick last night. I was home.' Her voice was a cautious throaty sound that just reached my ears.

'Like hell you were.'

Her eyes flicked up and down very swiftly.

'Before you went home,' I said. 'Before I took you home. Here. In that chair' – I pointed to it – 'on that orange shawl. You remember all right.'

A slow flush crept up her throat. That was something. She could blush. A glint of white showed under the clogged grey irises. She chewed hard on her thumb.

'You – were the one?' she whispered.

'Me. How much of it stays with you?'

She said vaguely: 'Are you the police?'

'No. I'm a friend of your father's.'

'You're not the police?'

'No.'

She let out a thin sigh. 'Wha– what do you want?'

'Who killed him?'

Her shoulders jerked, but nothing more moved in her face. 'Who else – knows?'

'About Geiger? I don't know. Not the police, or they'd be camping here. Maybe Joe Brody.'

It was a stab in the dark but it got her. 'Joe Brody! Him!'

Then we were both silent. I dragged at my cigarette and she ate her thumb.

'Don't get clever, for God's sake,' I urged her. 'This is a spot for a little old-fashioned simplicity. Did Brody kill him?'

'Kill who?'

'Oh, Christ,' I said.

She looked hurt. Her chin came down an inch. 'Yes,' she said solemnly. 'Joe did it.'

'Why?'

'I don't know.' She shook her head, persuading herself that she didn't know.

'Seen much of him lately?'

Her hands went down and made small white knots. 'Just once or twice. I hate him.'

'Then you know where he lives.'

'Yes.'

'And you don't like him any more?'

'I hate him!'

'Then you'd like him for the spot.'

A little blank again. I was going too fast for her. It was hard not to. 'Are you willing to tell the police it was Joe Brody?' I probed.

Sudden panic flamed all over her face. 'If I can kill the nude photo angle, of course,' I added soothingly.

She giggled. That gave me a nasty feeling. If she had screeched or wept or even nose-dived to the floor in a dead faint, that would have been all right. She just giggled. It was suddenly a lot of fun. She had had her photo taken as Isis and somebody had swiped it and somebody had bumped Geiger off in front of her and she was drunker than a Legion convention, and it was suddenly a lot of nice clean fun. So she giggled. Very cute. The giggles got louder and ran around the corners of the room like rats behind the wainscoting. She started to go hysterical. I slid off the desk and stepped up close to her and gave her a smack on the side of the face.

'Just like last night,' I said. 'We're a scream together. Reilly and Sternwood, two stooges in search of a comedian.'

The giggles stopped dead, but she didn't mind the slap any more than last night. Probably all her boy friends got around to slapping her sooner or later. I could understand how they might. I sat down on the end of the black desk again.

'Your name isn't Reilly,' she said seriously. 'It's Philip Marlowe. You're a private detective. Viv told me. She showed me your card.' She smoothed the cheek I had slapped. She smiled at me, as if I was nice to be with.

'Well, you do remember,' I said. 'And you came back to look for that photo and you couldn't get into the house. Didn't you?'

Her chin ducked down and up. She worked the smile. I was having the eye put on me. I was being brought into camp. I was going to yell 'Yippee!' in a minute and ask her to go to Yuma.

'The photo's gone,' I said. 'I looked last night, before I took you home. Probably Brody took it with him. You're not kidding me about Brody?'

She shook her head earnestly.

'It's a pushover,' I said. 'You don't have to give it another thought. Don't tell a soul you were here, last night or to-day. Not even Vivian. Just forget you were here. Leave it to Reilly.'

'Your name isn't –' she began, and then stopped and shook her head vigorously in agreement with what I had said or with what she had just thought of. Her eyes became narrow and almost black and as shallow as enamel on a cafeteria tray. She had had an idea. 'I have to go home now,' she said, as if we had been having a cup of tea.

'Sure.'

I didn't move. She gave me another cute glance and went on towards the front door. She had her hand on the knob when we both heard a car coming. She looked at me with questions in her eyes. I shrugged. The car stopped, right in front of the house. Terror twisted her face. There were steps and the bell rang. Carmen stared back at me over her shoulder, her hand clutching the door knob, almost drooling with fear. The bell kept on ringing. Then the ringing stopped. A key tickled at the door and Carmen jumped away from it and stood frozen. The door swung open. A man stepped through it briskly and stopped dead, staring at us quietly, with complete composure.

13

He was a grey man, all grey, except for his polished black shoes and two scarlet diamonds in his grey satin tie that looked like the diamonds on roulette layouts. His shirt was grey and his double-breasted suit of soft, beautifully-cut flannel. Seeing Carmen he took a grey hat off and his hair underneath it was grey and as fine as if it had been sifted through gauze. His thick grey eyebrows had that indefinably sporty look. He had a long chin, a nose with a hook to it, thoughtful grey eyes that had a slanted look because the fold of skin over his upper lid came down over the corner of the lid itself.

He stood there politely, one hand touching the door at his back, the other holding the grey hat and flapping it gently against his thigh. He looked hard, not the hardness of the tough guy. More like the hardness of a well-weathered horseman. But he was no horseman. He was Eddie Mars.

He pushed the door shut behind him and put that hand in the lap-seamed pocket of his coat and left the thumb outside to glisten in the rather dim light of the room. He smiled at Carmen. He had a nice easy smile. She licked her lips and stared at him. The fear went out of her face. She smiled back.

'Excuse the casual entrance,' he said. 'The bell didn't seem to rouse anybody. Is Mr Geiger around?'

I said: 'No. We don't know just where he is. We found the door a little open. We stepped inside.'

He nodded and touched his long chin with the brim of his hat. 'You're friends of his, of course?'

'Just business acquaintances. We dropped by for a book.'

'A book, eh?' He said that quickly and brightly and, I thought, a little slyly, as if he knew all about Geiger's books. Then he looked at Carmen again and shrugged.

I moved towards the door. 'We'll trot along now,' I said. I took hold of her arm. She was staring at Eddie Mars. She liked him.

'Any message – if Geiger comes back?' Eddie Mars asked gently.

'We won't bother you.'

'That's too bad,' he said, with too much meaning. His grey eyes twinkled and then hardened as I went past him to open the door. He added in a casual tone: 'The girl can dust. I'd like to talk to you a little, soldier.'

I let go of her arm. I gave him a blank stare. 'Kidder, eh?' he said nicely. 'Don't waste it. I've got two boys outside in a car that always do just what I want them to.'

Carmen made a sound at my side and bolted through the door. Her steps faded rapidly downhill. I hadn't seen her car, so she must have left it down below. I started to say: 'What the hell –!'

'Oh, skip it,' Eddie Mars sighed. 'There's something wrong around here. I'm going to find out what it is. If you want to pick lead out of your belly, get in my way.'

'Well, well,' I said, 'a tough guy.'

'Only when necessary, soldier.' He wasn't looking at me any more. He was walking around the room, frowning, not paying any attention to me. I looked out above the broken pane of the front window. The top of a car showed over the hedge. Its motor idled.

Eddie Mars found the purple flagon and the two gold-veined glasses on the desk. He sniffed at one of the glasses, then at the flagon. A disgusted smile wrinkled his lips. 'The lousy pimp,' he said tonelessly.

He looked at a couple of books, grunted, went on around the desk and stood in front of the little totem pole with the camera eye. He studied it, dropped his glance to the floor in front of it. He moved the small rug with his foot, then bent swiftly, his body tense. He went down on the floor with one grey knee. The desk hid him from me partly. There was a sharp exclamation and he came up again. His arm flashed under his coat and a black Luger appeared in his hand. He held it in long brown fingers, not pointing it at me, not pointing it at anything.

'Blood,' he said. 'Blood on the floor there, under the rug. Quite a lot of blood.'

'Is that so?' I said, looking interested.

He slid into the chair behind the desk and hooked the mulberry-coloured phone towards him and shifted the Luger to his left hand. He frowned sharply at the telephone, bringing his thick grey eyebrows close together and making a hard crease in the weathered skin at the top of his hooked nose. 'I think we'll have some law,' he said.

I went over and kicked at the rug that lay where Geiger had lain. 'It's old blood,' I said. 'Dried blood.'

'Just the same we'll have some law.'

'Why not?' I said.

His eyes went narrow. The veneer had flaked off him, leaving a well-dressed hard boy with a Luger. He didn't like my agreeing with him.

'Just who the hell are you, soldier?'

'Marlowe is the name. I'm a sleuth.'

'Never heard of you. Who's the girl?'

'Client. Geiger was trying to throw a loop on her with some blackmail. We came to talk it over. He wasn't here. The door being open we walked in to wait. Or did I tell you that?'

'Convenient,' he said. 'The door being open. When you didn't have a key.'

'Yes. How come *you* had a key?'

'Is that any of your business, soldier?'

'I could make it my business.'

He smiled tightly and pushed his hat back on his grey hair. 'And I could make your business my business.'

'You wouldn't like it. The pay's too small.'

'All right, bright eyes. I own this house. Geiger is my tenant. Now what do you think of that?'

'You know such lovely people.'

'I take them as they come. They come all kinds.' He glanced down at the Luger, shrugged and tucked it back under his arm. 'Got any good ideas, soldier?'

'Lots of them. Somebody gunned Geiger. Somebody got gunned by Geiger, who ran away. Or it was two other fellows. Or Geiger was running a cult and made blood sacrifices in front of that totem pole. Or he had chicken for dinner and liked to kill his chickens in the front parlour.'

The grey man scowled at me.

'I give up,' I said. 'Better call your friends down-town.'

'I don't get it,' he said. 'I don't get your game here.'

'Go ahead, call the buttons. You'll get a big reaction from it.'

He thought that over without moving. His lips went back against his teeth. 'I don't get that, either,' he said tightly.

'Maybe it just isn't your day. I know you, Mr Mars. The Cypress Club at Las Olindas. Flash gambling for flash people. The local law in your pocket and a well-greased line into LA. In other words, protection. Geiger was in a racket that needed that too. Perhaps you spared him a little now and then, seeing he's your tenant.'

His mouth became a hard white grimace. 'Geiger was in what racket?'

'The smut book racket.'

He stared at me for a long level minute. 'Somebody got to him,' he said softly. 'You know something about it. He didn't show at the store to-day. They don't know where he is. He didn't answer the phone here. I came up to see about it. I find blood on the floor, under a rug. And you and a girl here.'

'A little weak,' I said. 'But maybe you can sell the story

to a willing buyer. You missed a little something, though. Somebody moved his books out of the store to-day – the nice books he rented out.'

He snapped his fingers sharply and said: 'I should have thought of that, soldier. You seem to get around. How do you figure it?'

'I think Geiger was rubbed. I think that is his blood. And the books being moved out gives a motive for hiding the body for a while. Somebody is taking over the racket and wants a little time to organize.'

'They can't get away with it,' Eddie Mars said grimly.

'Who says so? You and a couple of gunmen in your car outside? This is a big town now, Eddie. Some very tough people have checked in here lately. The penalty of growth.'

'You talk too damned much,' Eddie Mars said. He bared his teeth and whistled twice, sharply. A car door slammed outside and running steps came through the hedge. Mars flicked the Luger out again and pointed it at my chest. 'Open the door.'

The knob rattled and a voice called out. I didn't move. The muzzle of the Luger looked like the mouth of the Second Street tunnel, but I didn't move. Not being bullet-proof is an idea I had had to get used to.

'Open it yourself, Eddie. Who the hell are you to give me orders? Be nice and I might help you out.'

He came to his feet rigidly and moved around the end of the desk and over to the door. He opened it without taking his eyes off me. Two men tumbled into the room, reaching busily under their arms. One was an obvious pug, a good-looking pale-faced boy with a bad nose and one ear like a club steak. The other man was slim, blonde, deadpan, with close-set eyes and no colour in them.

Eddie Mars said: 'See if this bird is wearing any iron.'

The blonde flicked a short-barrelled gun out and stood pointing it at me. The pug sidled over flatfooted and felt my pockets with care. I turned around for him like a bored beauty modelling an evening gown.

'No gun,' he said in a burry voice.

'Find out who he is.'

The pug slipped a hand into my breast pocket and drew out my wallet. He flipped it open and studied the contents. 'Name's Philip Marlowe, Eddie. Lives at the Hobart Arms on Franklin. Private licence, deputy's badge and all. A shamus.' He slipped the wallet back in my pocket, slapped my face lightly and turned away.

'Beat it,' Eddie Mars said.

The two gunmen went out again and closed the door. There was the sound of them getting back into the car. They started its motor and kept it idling once more.

'All right. Talk,' Eddie Mars said. The peaks of his eyebrows made sharp angles against his forehead.

'I'm not ready to give out. Killing Geiger to grab his racket would be a dumb trick and I'm not sure it happened that way, assuming he has been killed. But I'm sure that whoever got the books knows what's what, and I'm sure that the blonde lady down at his store is scared batty about something or other. And I have a guess who got the books.'

'Who?'

'That's the part I'm not ready to give out. I've got a client, you know.'

He wrinkled his nose. 'That – ' he chopped it off quickly.

'I expected you would know the girl,' I said.

'Who got the books, soldier?'

'Not ready to talk, Eddie. Why should I?'

He put the Luger down on the desk and slapped it with his open palm. 'This,' he said. 'And I might make it worth your while.'

'That's the spirit. Leave the gun out of it. I can always hear the sound of money. How much are you clinking at me?'

'For doing what?'

'What did you want done?'

He slammed the desk hard. 'Listen, soldier. I ask you a question and you ask me another. We're not getting anywhere. I want to know where Geiger is, for my own personal reasons. I didn't like his racket and I didn't protect him. I happen to own this house. I'm not so crazy about that right now. I can believe that whatever you know about all this is under glass, or there would be a flock of johns squeaking sole leather around this dump. You haven't got anything to sell. My guess is you need a little protection yourself. So cough up.'

It was a good guess, but I wasn't going to let him know it. I lit a cigarette and blew the match out and flicked it at the glass eye of the totem pole. 'You're right,' I said. 'If anything has happened to Geiger, I'll have to give what I have to the law. Which puts it in the public domain and doesn't leave me anything to sell. So with your permission I'll just drift.'

His face whitened under the tan. He looked mean, fast and tough for a moment. He made a movement to lift the gun. I added casually: 'By the way, how is Mrs Mars these days?'

I thought for a moment I had kidded him a little too far. His hand jerked at the gun, shaking. His face was stretched out by hard muscles. 'Beat it,' he said quite softly. 'I don't give a damn where you go or what you do when you get there. Only take a word of advice, soldier. Leave me out of your plans or you'll wish your name was Murphy and you lived in Limerick.'

'Well, that's not so far from Clonmel,' I said. 'I hear you had a pal came from there.'

He leaned down on the desk, frozen-eyed, unmoving. I went over to the door and opened it and looked back at him. His eyes had followed me, but his lean grey body had not moved. There was hate in his eyes. I went out and through the hedge and up the hill to my car and got into it. I turned it around and drove up over the crest. Nobody shot at me. After a few blocks I turned off, cut the motor and sat for a few moments. Nobody followed me either. I drove back into Hollywood.

14

It was ten minutes to five when I parked near the lobby entrance of the apartment house on Randall Place. A few windows were lit and radios were bleating at the dusk. I rode the automatic elevator up to the fourth floor and went along a wide hall carpeted in green and panelled in ivory. A cool breeze blew down the hall from the open screened door to the fire escape.

There was a small ivory pushbutton beside the door marked '405'. I pushed it and waited what seemed a long time. Then the door opened noiselessly about a foot. There was a steady, furtive air in the way it opened. The man was long-legged, long-waisted, high-shouldered and he had dark brown eyes in a brown expressionless face that had learned to control its expressions long ago. Hair like steel wool grew far back on his head and gave him a great deal of domed brown forehead that might at a careless glance have seemed a dwelling-place for brains. His sombre eyes probed at me impersonally. His long thin brown fingers held the edge of the door. He said nothing.

I said: 'Geiger?'

Nothing in the man's face changed that I could see. He

brought a cigarette from behind the door and tucked it between his lips and drew a little smoke from it. The smoke came towards me in a lazy, contemptuous puff and behind it words in a cool, unhurried voice that had no more inflection than the voice of a faro dealer.

'You said what?'

'Geiger. Arthur Gwynn Geiger. The guy that has the books.'

The man considered that without any haste. He glanced down at the tip of his cigarette. His other hand, the one that had been holding the door, dropped out of sight. His shoulder had a look as though his hidden hand might be making motions.

'Don't know anybody by that name,' he said. 'Does he live around here?'

I smiled. He didn't like the smile. His eyes got nasty. I said: 'You're Joe Brody?'

The brown face hardened. 'So what? Got a grift, brother – or just amusing yourself?'

'So you're Joe Brody,' I said. 'And you don't know anybody named Geiger. That's very funny.'

'Yeah? You got a funny sense of humour maybe. Take it away and play on it somewhere else.'

I leaned against the door and gave him a dreamy smile. 'You got the books, Joe. I got the sucker list. We ought to talk things over.'

He didn't shift his eyes from my face. There was a faint sound in the room behind him, as though a metal curtain ring clicked lightly on a metal rod. He glanced sideways into the room. He opened the door wider.

'Why not – if you think you've got something?' he said coolly. He stood aside from the door. I went past him into the room.

It was a cheerful room with good furniture and not too much of it. French windows in the end wall opened on a stone porch and looked across the dusk at the foothills. Near the windows a closed door in the west wall and near the entrance door another door in the same wall. This last had a plush curtain drawn across it on a thin brass rod below the lintel.

That left the east wall, in which there were no doors. There was a davenport backed against the middle of it, so I sat down on the davenport. Brody shut the door and walked crab-fashion to a tall oak desk studded with square nails. A cedarwood box with gilt hinges lay on the lower leaf of the desk. He carried the box to an easy chair midway between the other two doors and sat down. I dropped my hat on the davenport and waited.

'Well, I'm listening,' Brody said. He opened the cigar box and dropped his cigarette stub into a dish at his side. He put a long thin cigar in his mouth. 'Cigar?' He tossed one at me through the air.

I reached for it. Brody took a gun out of the cigar box and pointed it at my nose. I looked at the gun. It was a black Police .38. I had no argument against it at the moment.

'Neat, huh?' Brody said. 'Just kind of stand up a minute. Come forward just about two yards. You might grab a little air while you're doing that.' His voice was the elaborately casual voice of the tough guy in pictures. Pictures have made them all like that.

'Tsk, tsk,' I said, not moving at all. 'Such a lot of guns around town and so few brains. You're the second guy I've met within hours who seems to think a gat in the hand means a world by the tail. Put it down and don't be silly, Joe.'

His eyebrows came together and he pushed his chin at me. His eyes were mean.

'The other guy's name is Eddie Mars,' I said. 'Ever heard of him?'

'No.' Brody kept the gun pointed at me.

'If he ever gets wise to where you were last night in the rain, he'll wipe you off the way a check raiser wipes a check.'

'What would I be to Eddie Mars?' Brody asked coldly. But he lowered the gun to his knee.

'Not even a memory,' I said.

We stared at each other. I didn't look at the pointed black slipper that showed under the plush curtain on the doorway to my left.

Brody said quietly: 'Don't get me wrong. I'm not a tough guy – just careful. I don't know hell's first whisper about you. You might be a lifetaker for all I know.'

'You're not careful enough,' I said. 'That play with Geiger's books was terrible.'

He drew a long slow breath and let it out silently. Then he leaned back and crossed his long legs and held the Colt on his knee.

'Don't kid yourself I won't use this heat, if I have to,' he said. 'What's your story?'

'Have your friend with the pointed slippers come on in. She gets tired of holding her breath.'

Brody called out without moving his eyes off my stomach. 'Come on in, Agnes.'

The curtain swung aside and the green-eyed, thigh-swinging ash blonde from Geiger's store joined us in the room. She looked at me with a kind of mangled hatred. Her nostrils were pinched and her eyes had darkened a couple of shades. She looked very unhappy.

'I knew damn well you were trouble,' she snapped at me. 'I told Joe to watch his step.'

'It's not his step, it's the back of his lap he ought to watch,' I said.

'I suppose that's funny,' the blonde said.

'It has been,' I said. 'But it probably isn't any more.'

'Save the gags,' Brody advised me. 'Joe's watchin' his step plenty. Put some light on so I can see to pop this guy, if it works out that way.'

The blonde snicked on a light in a big square standing lamp. She sank down into a chair beside the lamp and sat stiffly, as if her girdle was too tight. I put my cigar in my mouth and bit the end off. Brody's Colt took a close interest in me while I got matches out and lit the cigar. I tasted the smoke and said:

'The sucker list I spoke of is in code. I haven't cracked it yet, but there are about five hundred names. You got twelve boxes of books that I know of. You should have at least five hundred books. There'll be a bunch more out on loan, but say five hundred is the full crop, just to be cautious. If it's a good active list and you could run it even fifty per cent down the line, that would be one hundred and twenty-five thousand rentals. Your girl friend knows all about that. I'm only guessing. Put the average rental as low as you like, but it won't be less than a dollar. That merchandise costs money. At a dollar a rental you take one hundred and twenty-five grand and you still have your capital. I mean, you still have Geiger's capital. That's enough to spot a guy for.'

The blonde said: 'You're crazy, you goddam egg-headed – !'

Brody put his teeth sideways at her and snarled: 'Pipe down, for Chrissake. Pipe down!'

She subsided into an outraged mixture of slow anguish and bottled fury. Her silvery nails scraped on her knees.

'It's no racket for bums,' I told Brody almost affectionately. 'It takes a smooth worker like you, Joe. You've got to get confidence and keep it. People who spend their money for second-hand sex jags are as nervous as dowagers who can't find the rest-room. Personally I think the blackmail angles are a big mistake. I'm for shedding all that and sticking to legitimate sales and rentals.'

Brody's dark brown stare moved up and down my face. His Colt went on hungering for my vital organs. 'You're a funny guy,' he said tonelessly. 'Who has this lovely racket?'

'*You* have,' I said. 'Almost.'

The blonde choked and clawed her ear. Brody didn't say anything. He just looked at me.

'What?' the blonde called. 'You sit there and try to tell us Mr Geiger ran that kind of business right down on the main drag? You're nuts!'

I leered at her politely. 'Sure I do. Everybody knows the racket exists. Hollywood's made to order for it. If a thing like that has to exist, then right out on the street is where all practical coppers want it to exist. For the same reason they favour red light districts. They know where to flush the game when they want to.'

'My God,' the blonde said. 'You let this cheese-head sit there and insult me, Joe? You with a gun in your hand and him holding nothing but a cigar and his thumb?'

'I like it,' Brody said. 'The guy's got good ideas. Shut your trap and keep it shut, or I'll slap it shut for you with this.' He flicked the gun around in an increasingly negligent manner.

The blonde gasped and turned her face to the wall. Brody looked at me and said cunningly: '*How* have I got that lovely racket?'

'You shot Geiger to get it. Last night in the rain. It was dandy shooting weather. The trouble is he wasn't alone when you whiffed him. Either you didn't notice that, which seems unlikely, or you got the wind up and lammed. But you had nerve enough to take the plate out of his camera and you had nerve enough to come back later on and hide his corpse, so you could tidy up on the books before the law knew it had a murder to investigate.'

'Yah,' Brody said contemptuously. The Colt wobbled on his knee. His brown face was as hard as a piece of carved wood. 'You take chances, mister. It's kind of goddamned lucky for you I *didn't* bop Geiger.'

'You can step off for it just the same,' I told him cheerfully. 'You're made to order for the rap.'

Brody's voice went rough. 'Think you got me framed for it?'

'Positive.'

'How come?'

'There's somebody who'll tell it that way. I told you there was a witness. Don't go simple on me, Joe.'

He exploded then. 'That goddamned little hot pants!' he shouted. 'She would, goddamn her! She would – just that!'

I leaned back and grinned at him. 'Swell. I thought you had those nude photos of her.'

He didn't say anything. The blonde didn't say anything. I let them chew on it. Brody's face cleared slowly, with a sort of greyish relief. He put his Colt down on the end table beside his chair but kept his right hand close to it. He knocked ash from his cigar on the carpet and stared at me with eyes that were a tight shine between narrowed lids.

'I guess you think I'm dumb,' Brody said.

'Just average, for a grifter. Get the pictures.'

'What pictures?'

I shook my head. 'Wrong play, Joe. Innocence gets you nowhere. You were either there last night, or you got the nude photo from somebody that was there. You know *she* was there because you had your girl friend threaten Mrs Regan with a police rap. The only ways you could know enough to do that would be by seeing what happened or by holding the photo and knowing where and when it was taken. Cough up and be sensible.'

'I'd have to have a little dough,' Brody said. He turned his head a little to look at the green-eyed blonde. Not now green-eyed and only superficially a blonde. She was as limp as a fresh-killed rabbit.

'No dough,' I said.

He scowled bitterly. 'How d'you get to me?'

I flicked my wallet out and let him look at my buzzer. 'I was working on Geiger – for a client. I was outside last night, in the rain. I heard the shots. I crashed in. I didn't see the killer. I saw everything else.'

'And kept your lip buttoned,' Brody sneered.

I put my wallet away. 'Yes,' I admitted. 'Up till now. Do I get the photos or not?'

'About these books,' Brody said. 'I don't get that.'

'I tailed them here from Geiger's store. I have a witness.'

'That punk kid?'

'What punk kid?'

He scowled again. 'The kid that works at the store. He skipped out after the truck left. Agnes don't even know where he flops.'

'That helps,' I said, grinning at him. 'That angle worried me a little. Either of you ever been in Geiger's house – before last night?'

'Not even last night,' Brody said sharply. 'So she says I gunned him, eh?'

'With the photos in hand I might be able to convince her she was wrong. There was a little drinking being done.'

Brody sighed. 'She hates my guts. I bounced her out. I got paid, sure, but I'd have had to do it anyway. She's too screwy for a simple guy like me.' He cleared his throat. 'How about a little dough? I'm down to nickels. Agnes and me gotta move on.'

'Not from my client.'

'Listen –'

'Get the pictures, Brody.'

'Oh, hell,' he said. 'You win.' He stood up and slipped the Colt into his side pocket. His left hand went up inside his coat. He was holding it there, his face twisted with disgust, when the door buzzer rang and kept on ringing.

15

He didn't like that. His lower lip went in under his teeth, and his eyebrows drew down sharply at the corners. His whole face became sharp and foxy and mean.

The buzzer kept up its song. I didn't like it either. If the visitors should happen to be Eddie Mars and his boys, I might get chilled off just for being there. If it was the police, I was caught with nothing to give them but a smile and a promise. And if it was some of Brody's friends – supposing he had any – they might turn out to be tougher than he was.

The blonde didn't like it. She stood up in a surge and chipped at the air with one hand. Nerve tension made her face old and ugly.

Watching me, Brody jerked a small drawer in the desk and picked a bone-handled automatic out of it. He held it at the blonde. She slid over to him and took it, shaking.

'Sit down next to him,' Brody said. 'Hold it on him low down, away from the door. If he gets funny use your own judgment. We ain't licked yet, baby.'

'Oh, Joe,' the blonde wailed. She came over and sat next to me on the davenport and pointed the gun at my leg artery. I didn't like the jerky look in her eyes.

The door buzzer stopped humming and a quick impatient rapping on the wood followed it. Brody put his hand in his pocket, on his gun, and walked over to the door and opened it with his left hand. Carmen Sternwood pushed him back into the room by putting a little revolver against his lean brown lips.

Brody backed away from her with his mouth working and an expression of panic on his face. Carmen shut the door behind her and looked neither at me nor at Agnes. She stalked Brody carefully, her tongue sticking out a little between her teeth. Brody took both hands out of his pockets and gestured placatingly at her. His eyebrows designed themselves into an odd assortment of curves and angles. Agnes turned the gun away from me and swung it at Carmen. I shot my hand out and closed my fingers down hard over her hand and jammed my thumb on the safety catch. It was already on. I kept it on. There was a short silent tussle, to which neither Brody nor Carmen paid any attention whatever. I had the gun. Agnes breathed deeply and shivered the whole length of her body. Carmen's face had a bony scraped look and her breath hissed. Her voice said without tone:

'I want my pictures, Joe.'

Brody swallowed and tried to grin. 'Sure, kid, sure.' He said it in a small flat voice that was as much like the voice he had used to me as a scooter is like a ten-ton truck.

Carmen said: 'You shot Arthur Geiger. I saw you. I want my pictures.' Brody turned green.

'Hey, wait a minute, Carmen,' I called.

Blonde Agnes came to life with a rush. She ducked her head and sank her teeth in my right hand. I made more noises and shook her off.

'Listen, kid,' Brody said. 'Listen a minute –'

The blonde spat at me and threw herself on my leg and tried to bite that. I cracked her on the head with the gun, not very hard, and tried to stand up. She rolled down my legs and wrapped her arms around them. I fell back on the davenport. The blonde was strong with the madness of love or fear, or a mixture of both, or maybe she was just strong.

Brody grabbed for the little revolver that was so close to his face. He missed. The gun made a sharp rapping noise that was not very loud. The bullet broke glass in a folded-back French window. Brody groaned horribly and fell down on the floor and jerked Carmen's feet from under her. She landed in a heap and the little revolver went skidding off into a corner. Brody jumped up on his knees and reached for his pocket.

I hit Agnes on the head with less delicacy than before, kicked her off my feet, and stood up. Brody flicked his eyes at me. I showed him the automatic. He stopped trying to get his hand into his pocket.

'Christ!' he whined. 'Don't let her kill me!'

I began to laugh. I laughed like an idiot, without control. Blonde Agnes was sitting up on the floor with her hands flat on the carpet and her mouth wide open and a wick of metallic blonde hair down over her right eye. Carmen was crawling on her hands and knees, still hissing. The metal of her little revolver glistened against the baseboard over in the corner. She crawled towards it relentlessly.

I waved my share of the guns at Brody and said: 'Stay put. You're all right.'

I stepped past the crawling girl and picked the gun up. She looked at me and began to giggle. I put her gun in my pocket and patted her on the back. 'Get up, angel. You look like a Pekinese.'

I went over to Brody and put the automatic against his midriff and reached his Colt out of his side pocket. I now had all the guns that had been exposed to view. I stuffed them into my pockets and held my hand out to him.

'Give.'

He nodded, licking his lips, his eyes still scared. He took a fat envelope out of his breast pocket and gave it to me. There was a developed plate in the envelope and five glossy prints.

'Sure these are all?'

He nodded again. I put the envelope in my own breast pocket and turned away. Agnes was back on the davenport, straightening her hair. Her eyes ate Carmen with a green distillation of hate. Carmen was up on her feet too, coming towards me with her hand out, still giggling and hissing. There was a little froth at the corners of her mouth. Her small white teeth glinted close to her lips.

'Can I have them now?' she asked me with a coy smile.

'I'll take care of them for you. Go on home.'

'Home?'

I went to the door and looked out. The cool night breeze was blowing peacefully down the hall. No excited neighbours hung out of doorways. A small gun had gone off and broken a pane of glass, but noises like that don't mean much any more. I held the door open and jerked my head at Carmen. She came towards me, smiling uncertainly.

'Go on home and wait for me,' I said soothingly.

She put her thumb up. Then she nodded and slipped past me into the hall. She touched my cheek with her fingers as she went by. 'You'll take care of Carmen, won't you?' she said.

'Check.'

'You're cute.'

'What you see is nothing,' I said. 'I've got a Bali dancing girl tattooed on my right thigh.'

Her eyes rounded. She said: 'Naughty,' and wagged a finger at me. Then she whispered: 'Can I have my gun?'

'Not now. Later. I'll bring it to you.'

She grabbed me suddenly around the neck and kissed me on the mouth. 'I like you,' she said. 'Carmen likes you a lot.' She ran off down the hall as gay as a thrush, waved at me from the stairs and ran down the stairs out of my sight.

I went back into Brody's apartment.

16

I went over to the folded-back French window and looked at the small broken pane in the upper part of it. The bullet from Carmen's gun had smashed the glass like a blow. It had not made a hole. There was a small hole in the plaster which a keen eye would find quickly enough. I pulled the drapes over the broken pane and took Carmen's gun out of my pocket. It was a Banker's Special, .22 calibre, hollow point cartridges. It had a pearl grip, and a small round silver plate set into the butt was engraved: 'Carmen from Owen'. She made saps of all of them.

I put the gun back in my pocket and sat down close to Brody and stared into his bleak brown eyes. A minute passed. The blonde adjusted her face by the aid of a pocket mirror. Brody fumbled around with a cigarette and jerked: 'Satisfied?'

'So far. Why did you put the bite on Mrs Regan instead of the old man?'

'Tapped the old man once. About six, seven months ago. I figure maybe he gets sore enough to call in some law.'

'What made you think Mrs Regan wouldn't tell him about it?'

He considered that with some care, smoking his cigarette and keeping his eyes on my face. Finally he said: 'How well you know her?'

'I've met her twice. You must know her a lot better to take a chance on that squeeze with the photo.'

'She skates around plenty. I figure maybe she has a couple of soft spots she don't want the old man to know about. I figure she can raise five grand easy.'

'A little weak,' I said. 'But pass it. You're broke, eh?'

'I been shaking two nickels together for a month, trying to get them to mate.'

'What you do for a living?'

'Insurance. I got desk rooms in Puss Walgreen's office, Fulwider Building, Western and Santa Monica.'

'When you open up, you open up. The books here in your apartment?'

He snapped his teeth and waved a brown hand. Confidence was oozing back into his manner. 'Hell, no. In storage.'

'You had a man bring them here and then you had a storage outfit come and take them away again right afterwards?'

'Sure. I don't want them moved direct from Geiger's place, do I?'

'You're smart,' I said admiringly. 'Anything incriminating in the joint right now?'

He looked worried again. He shook his head sharply.

'That's fine,' I told him. I looked across at Agnes. She had finished fixing her face and was staring at the wall, blank-eyed, hardly listening. Her face had the drowsiness which strain and shock induce, after their first incidence.

Brody flicked his eyes warily. 'Well?'

'How'd you come by the photo?'

He scowled. 'Listen, you got what you came after, got it plenty cheap. You done a nice neat job. Now go peddle it to your top man. I'm clean. I don't know nothing about any photo, do I, Agnes?'

The blonde opened her eyes and looked at him with vague but uncomplimentary speculation. 'A half-smart guy,' she said with a tired sniff. 'That's all I ever draw. Never once a guy that's smart all the way around the course. Never once.'

I grinned at her. 'Did I hurt your head much?'

'You and every other man I ever met.'

I looked back at Brody. He was pinching his cigarette between his fingers, with a sort of twitch. His hand seemed to be shaking a little. His brown poker face was still smooth.

'We've got to agree on a story,' I said. 'For instance, Carmen wasn't here. That's very important. She wasn't here. That was a vision you saw.'

'Huh!' Brody sneered. 'If you say so, pal, and if –' he put his hand out palm up and cupped the fingers and rolled the thumb gently against the index and middle fingers.

I nodded. 'We'll see. There might be a small contribution. You won't count it in grands, though. Now where did you get the picture?'

'A guy slipped it to me.'

'Uh-huh. A guy you just passed in the street. You wouldn't know him again. You never saw him before.'

Brody yawned. 'It dropped out of his pocket,' he said.

'Uh-huh. Got an alibi for last night, poker pan?'

'Sure. I was right here. Agnes was with me. Okey, Agnes?'

'I'm beginning to feel sorry for you again,' I said.

His eyes flicked wide and his mouth hung loose, the cigarette balanced on his lower lip.

'You think you're smart and you're so goddamned dumb,' I told him. 'Even if you don't dance off up in Quentin, you have such a bleak long lonely time ahead of you.'

His cigarette jerked and dropped ash on his waistcoat.

'Thinking about how smart you are,' I said.

'Take the air,' he growled suddenly. 'Dust. I got enough chinning with you. Beat it.'

'Okey.' I stood up and went over to the tall oak desk and took his two guns out of my pockets, laid them side by side on the blotter so that the barrels were exactly parallel. I reached my hat off the floor beside the davenport and started for the door.

Brody called: 'Hey!'

I turned and waited. His cigarette was jiggling like a doll on a coiled spring. 'Everything's smooth, ain't it?' he asked.

'Why, sure. This is a free country. You don't have to stay out of jail, if you don't want to. That is, if you're a citizen. Are you a citizen?'

He just stared at me, jiggling the cigarette. The blonde Agnes turned her head slowly and stared at me along the same level. Their glances contained almost the exact same blend of foxiness, doubt and frustrated anger. Agnes reached her silvery nails up abruptly and yanked a hair out of her head and broke it between her fingers with a bitter jerk.

Brody said tightly: 'You're not going to any cops, brother. Not if it's the Sternwoods you're working for. I've got too much stuff on that family. You got your pictures and you got your hush. Go and peddle your papers.'

'Make your mind up,' I said. 'You told me to dust, I was on my way out, you hollered at me and I stopped, and now I'm on my way out again. Is that what you want?'

'You ain't got anything on me,' Brody said.

'Just a couple of murders. Small change in your circle.'

He didn't jump more than an inch, but it looked like a foot. The white cornea showed all around the tobacco-coloured iris of his eyes. The brown skin of his face took on a greenish tinge in the lamplight.

Blonde Agnes let out a low animal wail and buried her head in a cushion on the end of the davenport. I stood there and admired the long line of her thighs.

Brody moistened his lips slowly and said: 'Sit down, pal. Maybe I have a little more for you. What's that crack about two murders mean?'

I leaned against the door. 'Where were you last night about seven-thirty, Joe?'

His mouth drooped sulkily and he stared down at the floor. 'I was watching a guy, a guy who had a nice racket I figured he needed a partner in. Geiger. I was watching him now and then to see had he any tough connections.

I figure he has friends or he don't work the racket as open as he does. But they don't go to his house. Only dames.'

'You didn't watch hard enough,' I said. 'Go on.'

'I'm there last night on the street below Geiger's house. It's raining hard and I'm buttoned up in my coupé and I don't see anything. There's a car in front of Geiger's and another car a little way up the hill. That's why I stay down below. There's a big Buick parked down where I am and after a while I go over and take a gander into it. It's registered to Vivian Regan. Nothing happens, so I scram. That's all.' He waved his cigarette. His eyes crawled up and down my face.

'Could be,' I said. 'Know where that Buick is now?'

'Why would I?'

'In the Sheriff's garage. It was lifted out of twelve feet of water off Lido fish pier this morning. There was a dead man in it. He had been sapped and the car pointed out the pier and the hand throttle pulled down.'

Brody was breathing hard. One of his feet tapped restlessly. 'Jesus, guy, you can't pin that one on me,' he said thickly.

'Why not? This Buick was down back of Geiger's according to you. Well, Mrs Regan didn't have it out. Her chauffeur, a lad named Owen Taylor, had it out. He went over to Geiger's place to have words with him, because Owen Taylor was sweet on Carmen, and he didn't like the kind of games Geiger was playing with her. He let himself in the back way with a jimmy and a gun and he caught Geiger taking a photo of Carmen without any clothes on. So his gun went off, as guns will, and Geiger fell down dead and Owen ran away, but not without the photo negative Geiger had just taken. So you ran after him and took the photo from him. How else would you have got hold of it?'

Brody licked his lips. 'Yeah,' he said. 'But that don't make me knock him off. Sure, I heard the shots and saw this killer come slamming down the back steps into the Buick and off. I took out after him. He hit the bottom of the canyon and went west on Sunset. Beyond Beverly Hills he skidded off the road and had to stop and I came up and played copper. He had a gun but his nerve was bad and I sapped him down. So I went through his clothes and found out who he was and I lifted the plateholder, just out of curiosity. I was wondering what it was all about and getting my neck wet when he came out of it all of a sudden and knocked me off the car. He was out of sight when I picked myself up. That's the last I saw of him.'

'How did you know it was Geiger he shot?' I asked gruffly.

Brody shrugged. 'I figure it was, but I can be wrong. When I had the plate developed and saw what was on it, I was pretty damn sure. And when Geiger didn't come down to the store this morning and didn't answer his phone I was plenty sure. So I figure it's a good time to move his books out and make a quick touch on the Sternwoods for travel money and blow for a while.'

I nodded. 'That seems reasonable. Maybe you didn't murder anybody at that. Where did you hide Geiger's body?'

He lifted his eyebrows. Then he grinned. 'Nix, nix. Skip it. You think I'd go back there and handle him, not knowing when a couple carloads of law would come tearing around the corner? Nix.'

'Somebody hid the body,' I said.

Brody shrugged. The grin stayed on his face. He didn't believe me. While he was still not believing me the door buzzer started to ring again. Brody stood up sharply, hard-eyed. He glanced over at his guns on the desk.

'So she's back again,' he growled.

'If she is, she doesn't have her gun,' I comforted him. 'Don't you have any other friends?'

'Just about one,' he growled. 'I got enough of this puss-in-the-corner game.' He marched to the desk and took the Colt. He held it down at his side and went to the door. He put his left hand to the knob and twisted it and opened the door a foot and leaned into the opening, holding the gun tight against his thigh.

A voice said: 'Brody?'

Brody said something I didn't hear. The two quick reports were muffled. The gun must have been pressed tight against Brody's body. He tilted forward against the door and the weight of his body pushed it shut with a bang. He slid down the wood. His feet pushed the carpet away behind him. His left hand dropped off the knob and the arm slapped the floor with a thud. His head was wedged against the door. He didn't move. The Colt clung to his right hand.

I jumped across the room and rolled him enough to get the door open and crowd through. A woman peered out of a door almost opposite. Her face was full of fright and she pointed along the hall with a clawlike hand.

I raced down the hall and heard thumping feet going down the tile steps and went down after the sound. At the lobby level the front door was closing itself quietly and running feet slapped the pavement outside. I made the door before it was shut, clawed it open again and charged out.

A tall hatless figure in a leather jerkin was running diagonally across the street between the parked cars. The figure turned and flame spurted from it. Two heavy hammers hit the stucco wall beside me. The figure ran on, dodged between two cars, vanished.

A man came up beside me and asked: 'What happened?'

'Shooting going on,' I said.

'Jesus!' He scuttled into the apartment house.

I walked quickly down the pavement to my car and got in and started it. I pulled out from the kerb and drove down the hill, not fast. No other car started up on the other side of the street. I thought I heard steps, but I wasn't sure about that. I rode down the hill a block and a half, turned at the intersection and started to back up. The sound of a muted whistling came to me faintly along the pavement. Then steps. I double parked and slid between two cars and went down low. I took Carmen's little revolver out of my pocket.

The sound of the steps grew louder, and the whistling went on cheerfully. In a moment the jerkin showed. I stepped out between the two cars and said: 'Got a match, buddy?'

The boy spun towards me and his right hand darted up to go inside the jerkin. His eyes were a wet shine in the glow of the round electroliers. Moist dark eyes shaped like almonds, and a pallid handsome face with wavy black hair growing low on the forehead in two points. A very handsome boy indeed, the boy from Geiger's store.

He stood there looking at me silently, his right hand on the edge of the jerkin, but not inside it yet. I held the little revolver down at my side.

'You must have thought a lot of that queen,' I said.

'Go – yourself,' the boy said softly, motionless between the parked cars and the five-foot retaining wall on the inside of the pavement.

A siren wailed distantly coming up the long hill. The boy's head jerked towards the sound. I stepped in close and put my gun into his jerkin.

'Me or the cops?' I asked him.

His head rolled a little sideways as if I had slapped his face. 'Who are you?' he said.

'Friend of Geiger's.'

'Get away from me, you son of a bitch.'

'This is a small gun, kid. I'll give it you through the navel and it will take three months to get you well enough to walk. But you'll get well. So you can walk to the nice new gas chamber up in Quentin.'

He said: 'Go – yourself.' His hand moved inside the jerkin. I pressed harder on his stomach. He let out a long soft sigh, took his hand away from the jerkin and let it fall limp at his side. His wide shoulders sagged. 'What you want?' he whispered.

I reached inside the jerkin and plucked out the automatic. 'Get into my car, kid.'

He stepped past me and I crowded him from behind. He got into the car.

'Under the wheel, kid. You drive.'

He slid under the wheel and I got into the car beside him. I said: 'Let the prowl car pass up the hill. They'll think we moved over when we heard the siren. Then turn her downhill and we'll go home.'

I put Carmen's gun away and leaned the automatic against the boy's ribs. I looked back through the window. The whine of the siren was very loud now. Two red lights swelled in the middle of the street. They grew larger and blended into one and the car rushed by in a wild flurry of sound.

'Let's go,' I said.

The boy swung the car and started off down the hill.

'Let's go home,' I said. 'To Laverne Terrace.'

His smooth lips twitched. He swung the car west on Franklin. 'You're a simple-minded lad. What's your name?'

'Carol Lundgren,' he said lifelessly.

'You shot the wrong guy, Carol. Joe Brody didn't kill your queen.'

He spoke three words to me and kept on driving.

17

A moon half gone from the full glowed through a ring of mist among the high branches of the eucalyptus trees on Laverne Terrace. A radio sounded loudly from a house low down the hill. The boy swung the car over to the box hedge in front of Geiger's house, killed the motor and sat looking straight before him with both hands on the wheel. No light showed through Geiger's hedge.

I said: 'Anybody home, son?'

'You ought to know.'

'How would I know?'

'Go – yourself.'

'That's how people get false teeth.'

He showed me his in a tight grin. Then kicked the door open and got out. I scuttled out after him. He stood with his fists on his hips, looking silently at the house above the top of the hedge.

'All right,' I said. 'You have a key. Let's go on in.'

'Who said I had a key?'

'Don't kid me, son. The fag gave you one. You've got a nice clean manly little room in there. He shooed you out and locked it up when he had lady visitors. He was like Caesar, a husband to women and a wife to men. Think I can't figure people like him and you out?'

I still held his automatic more or less pointed at him, but he swung on me just the same. It caught me flush on the chin. I backstepped fast enough to keep from falling, but I took plenty of the punch. It was meant to be a hard one, but a pansy has no iron in his bones, whatever he looks like.

I threw the gun down at the kid's feet and said: 'Maybe you need this.'

He stooped for it like a flash. There was nothing slow about his movements. I sank a fist in the side of his neck. He toppled over sideways, clawing for the gun and not reaching it. I picked it up again and threw it in the car. The boy came up on all fours, leering with his eyes too wide open. He coughed and shook his head.

'You don't want to fight,' I told him. 'You're giving away too much weight.'

He wanted to fight. He shot at me like a plane from a catapult, reaching for my knees in a diving tackle. I side-stepped and reached for his neck and took it into chancery. He scraped the dirt hard and got his feet under him enough to use his hands on me where it hurt. I twisted him around and heaved him a little higher. I took hold of my right wrist with my left hand and turned my right hipbone into him and for a moment it was a balance of weights. We seemed to hang there in the misty moonlight, two grotesque creatures whose feet scraped on the road and whose breath panted with effort.

I had my right forearm against his windpipe now and

all the strength of both arms in it. His feet began a frenetic shuffle and he wasn't panting any more. He was ironbound. His left foot sprawled off to one side and the knee went slack. I held on half a minute longer. He sagged on my arm, an enormous weight I could hardly hold up. Then I let go. He sprawled at my feet, out cold. I went to the car and got a pair of handcuffs out of the glove compartment and twisted his wrists behind him and snapped them on. I lifted him by the armpits and managed to drag him in behind the hedge, out of sight from the street. I went back to the car and moved it a hundred feet up the hill and locked it.

He was still out when I got back. I unlocked the door, dragged him into the house, shut the door. He was beginning to gasp now. I switched a lamp on. His eyes fluttered open and focused on me slowly.

I bent down, keeping out of the way of his knees and said: 'Keep quiet or you'll get the same and more of it. Just lie quiet and hold your breath. Hold it until you can't hold it any longer and then tell yourself that you have to breathe, that you're black in the face, that your eyeballs are popping out, and that you're going to breathe right now, but that you're sitting strapped in the chair in the clean little gas chamber up in San Quentin and when you take that breath you're fighting with all your soul not to take it, it won't be air you'll get, it will be cyanide fumes. And that's what they call humane execution in our state now.'

'Go – yourself,' he said with a soft stricken sigh.

'You're going to cop a plea, brother, don't ever think

you're not. And you're going to say just what we want you to say and nothing we don't want you to say.'

'Go – yourself.'

'Say that again and I'll put a pillow under your head.'

His mouth twitched. I left him lying on the floor with his wrists shackled behind him and his cheek pressed into the rug and an animal brightness in his visible eye. I put on another lamp and stepped into the hallway at the back of the living-room. Geiger's bedroom didn't seem to have been touched. I opened the door, not locked now, of thc bedroom across the hall from it. There was a dim flickering light in the room and a smell of sandalwood. Two cones of incense ash stood side by side on a small brass tray on the bureau. The light came from the two tall black candles in the foot-high candlesticks. They were standing on straight-backed chairs, one on either side of the bed.

Geiger lay on the bed. The two missing strips of Chinese tapestry made a St Andrew's Cross over the middle of his body, hiding the blood-smeared front of his Chinese coat. Below the cross his black-pyjama'd legs lay stiff and straight. His feet were in the slippers with thick white felt soles. Above the cross his arms were crossed at the wrists and his hands lay flat against his shoulders, palms down, fingers close together and stretched out evenly. His mouth was closed and his Charlie Chan moustache was as unreal as a toupee. His broad nose was pinched and white. His eyes were almost closed, but not entirely. The faint glitter of his glass eye caught the light and winked at me.

I didn't touch him. I didn't go very near him. He would be as cold as ice and as stiff as a board.

The black candles guttered in the draught from the open door. Drops of black wax crawled down their sides. The air of the room was poisonous and unreal. I went out and shut the door again and went back to the living-room. The boy hadn't moved. I stood still, listening for sirens. It was all a question of how soon Agnes talked and what she said. If she talked about Geiger, the police would be there any minute. But she might not talk for hours. She might even have got away.

I looked down at the boy. 'Want to sit up, son?'

He closed his eyes and pretended to go to sleep. I went over to the desk and scooped up the mulberry-coloured phone and dialled Bernie Ohls's office. He had left to go home at six o'clock. I dialled the number of his home. He was there.

'This is Marlowe,' I said. 'Did your boys find a revolver on Owen Taylor this morning?'

I could hear him clearing his throat and then I could hear him trying to keep the surprise out of his voice. 'That would come under the heading of police business,' he said.

'If they did, it had three empty shells in it.'

'How the hell did you know that?' Ohls asked quietly.

'Come over to 7244 Laverne Terrace, off Laurel Canyon Boulevard. I'll show you where the slugs went.'

'Just like that, huh?'

'Just like that.'

Ohls said: ‘Look out the window and you’ll see me coming round the corner. I thought you acted a little cagey on that one.’

‘Cagey is no word for it,’ I said.

18

Ohls stood looking down at the boy. The boy sat on the couch leaning sideways against the wall. Ohls looked at him silently, his pale eyebrows bristling and stiff and round like the little vegetable brushes the Fuller Brush man gives away.

He asked the boy: 'Do you admit shooting Brody?'

The boy said his favourite three words in a muffled voice.

Ohls sighed and looked at me. I said: 'He doesn't have to admit that. I have his gun.'

Ohls said: 'I wish to Christ I had a dollar for every time I've had that said to me. What's funny about it?'

'It's not meant to be funny,' I said.

'Well, that's something,' Ohls said. He turned away. 'I've called Wilde. We'll go over and see him and take this punk. He can ride with me and you can follow on behind in case he tries to kick me in the face.'

'How do you like what's in the bedroom?'

'I like it fine,' Ohls said. 'I'm kind of glad that Taylor kid went off the pier. I'd hate to have to help send him to the death-house for rubbing that skunk.'

I went back into the small bedroom and blew out the black candles and let them smoke. When I got back to the living-room Ohls had the boy up on his feet. The boy stood glaring at him with sharp black eyes in a face as hard and white as cold mutton fat.

'Let's go,' Ohls said, and took him by the arms as if he didn't like touching him. I put the lamps out and followed them out of the house. We got into our cars and I followed Ohls's twin tail-lights down the long curving hill. I hoped this would be my last trip to Laverne Terrace.

Taggart Wilde, the District Attorney, lived at the corner of Fourth and Lafayette Park, in a white frame house the size of a carbarn, with red sandstone *porte-cochère* built on to one side and a couple of acres of soft rolling lawn in front. It was one of those solid old-fashioned houses which it used to be the thing to move bodily to new locations as the city grew westward. Wilde came of an old Los Angeles family and had probably been born in the house when it was on West Adams or Figueroa or St James's Park.

There were two cars in the driveway already, a big private sedan and a police car with a uniformed chauffeur who leaned smoking against his rear fender and admiring the moon. Ohls went over and spoke to him and the chauffeur looked in at the boy in Ohls's car.

We went up to the house and rang the bell. A slick-haired blonde man opened the door and led us down the hall and through a huge sunken living-room crowded with heavy dark furniture and along another hall on the far side of it. He knocked at a door and stepped inside, then held the door wide and we went into a panelled study with an open French door at the end and a view of dark garden and mysterious trees. A smell of wet earth and flowers came in at the window. There were large dim oils on the walls, easy chairs, books, a smell of good cigar smoke which blended with the smell of wet earth and flowers.

Taggart Wilde sat behind a desk, a middle-aged plump man with clear blue eyes that managed to have a friendly expression without really having any expression at all. He had a cup of black coffee in front of him and he held a dappled thin cigar between the neat careful fingers of his left hand. Another man sat at the corner of the desk in a blue leather chair, a cold-eyed hatchet-faced man, as lean as a rake and as hard as the manager of a loan office. His neat well-kept face looked as if it had been shaved within the hour. He wore a well-pressed brown suit and there was a black pearl in his tie. He had the long nervous fingers of a man with a quick brain. He looked ready for a fight.

Ohls pulled a chair up and sat down and said: 'Evening, Cronjager. Meet Phil Marlowe, a private eye who's in a jam.' Ohls grinned.

Cronjager looked at me without nodding. He looked me over as if he was looking at a photograph. Then he nodded his chin about an inch. Wilde said: 'Sit down, Marlowe. I'll try to handle Captain Cronjager, but you know how it is. This is a big city now.'

I sat down and lit a cigarette. Ohls looked at Cronjager and asked: 'What did you get on the Randall Place killing?'

The hatchet-faced man pulled one of his fingers until the knuckle cracked. He spoke without looking up. 'A stiff, two slugs in him. Two guns that hadn't been fired. Down on the street we got a blonde trying to start a car that didn't belong to her. Hers was right next to it, the same model. She acted rattled so the boys brought her in and she spilled. She was in there when this guy Brody got it. Claims she didn't see the killer.'

'That all?' Ohls asked.

Cronjager raised his eyebrows a little. 'Only happened about an hour ago. What did you expect – moving pictures of the killing?'

'Maybe a description of the killer,' Ohls said.

'A tall guy in a leather jerkin – if you call that a description.'

'He's outside in my heap,' Ohls said. 'Handcuffed. Marlowe put the arm on him for you. Here's his gun.' Ohls took the boy's automatic out of his pocket and laid it on a corner of Wilde's desk. Cronjager looked at the gun but didn't reach for it.

Wilde chuckled. He was leaning back and puffing his dappled cigar without letting go of it. He bent forward to sip from his coffee cup. He took a silk handkerchief from the breast pocket of the dinner-jacket he was wearing and touched his lips with it and tucked it away again.

'There's a couple more deaths involved,' Ohls said, pinching the soft flesh at the end of his chin.

Cronjager stiffened visibly. His surly eyes became points of steely light.

Ohls said: 'You heard about a car being lifted out of

the Pacific Ocean off Lido pier this morning with a dead guy in it?'

Cronjager said: 'No,' and kept on looking nasty.

'The dead guy in the car was chauffeur to a rich family,' Ohls said. 'The family was being blackmailed on account of one of the daughters. Mr Wilde recommended Marlowe to the family, through me. Marlowe played it kind of close to the waistcoat.'

'I love private dicks that play murders close to the waistcoat,' Cronjager said. 'You don't have to be so goddamned coy about it.'

'Yeah,' Ohls said. 'I don't have to be so goddamned coy about it. It's not so goddamned often I get a chance to be coy with a city copper. I spend most of my time telling them where to put their feet so they won't break an ankle.'

Cronjager whitened around the corners of his sharp nose. His breath made a soft hissing sound in the quiet room. He said very quietly: 'You haven't had to tell any of *my* men where to put their feet, smart guy.'

'We'll see about that,' Ohls said. 'This chauffeur I spoke of that's drowned off Lido shot a guy last night in your territory. A guy named Geiger who ran a dirty book racket in a store on Hollywood Boulevard. Geiger was living with the punk I got outside in my car. I mean living with him, if you get the idea.'

Cronjager was staring at him levelly now. 'That sounds like it might grow up to be a dirty story,' he said.

'It's my experience most police stories are,' Ohls growled and turned to me, his eyebrows bristling. 'You're on the air, Marlowe. Give it to him.'

I gave it to him.

I left out two things, not knowing just why, at the moment, I left out one of them. I left out Carmen's visit to Brody's apartment and Eddie Mars's visit to Geiger's in the afternoon. I told the rest of it just as it happened.

Cronjager never took his eyes off my face and no expression of any kind crossed his as I talked. At the end of it he was perfectly silent for a long minute. Wilde was silent, sipping his coffee, puffing gently at his dappled cigar. Ohls stared at one of his thumbs.

Cronjager leaned slowly back in his chair and crossed one ankle over his knee and rubbed the ankle-bone with his thin nervous hand. His lean face wore a harsh frown. He said with deadly politeness:

'So all you did was not report a murder that happened last night and then spend to-day foxing around so that this kid of Geiger's could commit a second murder this evening.'

'That's all,' I said. 'I was in a pretty tough spot. I guess I did wrong, but I wanted to protect my client and I hadn't any reason to think the boy would go gunning for Brody.'

'That kind of thinking is police business, Marlowe. If Geiger's death had been reported last night, the books could never have been moved from the store to Brody's apartment. The kid wouldn't have been led to Brody and wouldn't have killed him. Say Brody was living on borrowed time. His kind usually are. But a life is a life.'

'Right,' I said. 'Tell that to your coppers next time they shoot down some scared petty larceny crook running away up an alley with a stolen spare.'

Wilde put both his hands down on his desk with a solid smack. 'That's enough of that,' he snapped. 'What makes you so sure, Marlowe, that this Taylor boy shot Geiger? Even if the gun that killed Geiger was found on Taylor's body or in the car, it doesn't absolutely follow that he was the killer. The gun might have been planted – say by Brody, the actual killer.'

'It's physically possible,' I said, 'but morally impossible. It assumes too much coincidence and too much that's out of character for Brody and his girl, and out of character for what he was trying to do. I talked to Brody for a long time. He was a crook, but not a killer type. He had two guns, but he wasn't wearing either of them. He was trying to find a way to cut in on Geiger's racket, which naturally he knew all about from the girl. He says he was watching Geiger off and on to see if he had any tough backers. I believe him. To suppose he killed Geiger in order to get his books, then scrammed with the nude photo Geiger had just taken of Carmen Sternwood, then planted the gun on Owen Taylor and pushed Taylor into the ocean off Lido, is to suppose a hell of a lot too much. Taylor had the motive, jealous rage, and the opportunity to kill Geiger. He was out in one of the family cars without permission. He killed Geiger right in front of the girl, which Brody would never have done, even if he had been a killer. I can't see anybody with a purely commercial interest in Geiger doing that. But Taylor would have done it. The nude photo business was just what would have made him do it.'

Wilde chuckled and looked along his eyes at Cronjager.

Cronjager cleared his throat with a snort. Wilde asked: 'What's this business about hiding the body? I don't see the point of that.'

I said: 'The kid hasn't told us, but he must have done it. Brody wouldn't have gone into the house after Geiger was shot. The boy must have got home when I was away taking Carmen to her house. He was afraid of the police, of course, being what he is, and he probably thought it a good idea to have the body hidden until he had removed his effects from the house. He dragged it out of the front door, judging by the marks on the rug, and very likely put it in the garage. Then he packed up whatever belongings he had there and took them away. And later on, sometime in the night and before the body stiffened, he had a revulsion of feeling and thought he hadn't treated his dead friend very nicely. So he went back and laid him out on the bed. That's all guessing of course.'

Wilde nodded. 'Then this morning he goes down to the store as if nothing had happened and keeps his eyes open. And when Brody moved the books out he found out where they were going and assumed that whoever got them had killed Geiger just for that purpose. He may even have known more about Brody and the girl than they suspected. What do you think, Ohls?'

Ohls said: 'We'll find out – but that doesn't help Cronjager's troubles. What's eating him is all this happened last night and he's only just been rung in on it.'

Cronjager said sourly: 'I think I can find some way to deal with that angle too.' He looked at me sharply and immediately looked away again.

Wilde waved his cigar and said: 'Let's see the exhibits, Marlowe.'

I emptied my pockets and put the catch on his desk: the three notes and Geiger's card to General Sternwood, Carmen's photos, and the blue notebook with the code list of names and addresses. I had already given Geiger's keys to Ohls.

Wilde looked at what I gave him, puffing gently at his cigar. Ohls lit one of his own toy cigars and blew smoke peacefully at the ceiling. Cronjager leaned on the desk and looked at what I had given Wilde.

Wilde tapped the three notes signed by Carmen and said: 'I guess these were just a come-on. If General Sternwood paid them, it would be through fear of something worse. Then Geiger would have tightened the screws. Do you know what he was afraid of?' He was looking at me.

I shook my head.

'Have you told your story complete in all relevant details?'

'I left out a couple of personal matters. I intend to keep on leaving them out, Mr Wilde.'

Cronjager said: 'Hah!' and snorted with deep feeling.

'Why?' Wilde asked quietly.

'Because my client is entitled to that protection, short of anything but a Grand Jury. I have a licence to operate as a private detective. I suppose that word "private" has some meaning. The Hollywood Division has two murders on its hands, both solved. They have both killers. They have the motive, the instrument in each case. The blackmail angle has got to be suppressed, as far as the names of the parties are concerned.'

'Why?' Wilde asked again.

'That's okey,' Cronjager said dryly. 'We're glad to stooge for a shamus of his standing.'

I said: 'I'll show you.' I got up and went back out of the house to my car and got the book from Geiger's store out of it. The uniformed police driver was standing beside Ohls's car. The boy was inside it, leaning back sideways in the corner.

'Has he said anything?' I asked.

'He made a suggestion,' the copper said and spat. 'I'm letting it ride.'

I went back into the house, put the book on Wilde's desk and opened up the wrappings. Cronjager was using a telephone on the end of the desk. He hung up and sat down as I came in.

Wilde looked through the book, wooden-faced, closed it and pushed it towards Cronjager. Cronjager opened it, looked at a page or two, shut it quickly. A couple of red spots the size of half-dollars showed on his cheek-bones.

I said: 'Look at the stamped dates on the front end-paper.'

Cronjager opened the book again and looked at them. 'Well?'

'If necessary,' I said, 'I'll testify under oath that that book came from Geiger's store. The blonde, Agnes, will admit what kind of business the store did. It's obvious to anybody with eyes that that store is just a front for something. But the Hollywood police allowed it to operate, for their own reasons. I dare say the Grand Jury would like to know what those reasons are.'

Wilde grinned. He said: 'Grand Juries do ask those embarrassing questions sometimes – in a rather vain effort to find out just why cities are run as they are run.'

Cronjager stood up suddenly and put his hat on. 'I'm one against three here,' he snapped. 'I'm a homicide man. If this Geiger was running indecent literature, that's no skin off my nose. But I'm ready to admit it won't help my division any to have it washed over in the papers. What do you birds want?'

Wilde looked at Ohls. Ohls said calmly: 'I want to turn a prisoner over to you. Let's go.'

He stood up. Cronjager looked at him fiercely and stalked out of the room. Ohls went after him. The door closed again. Wilde tapped on his desk and stared at me with his clear blue eyes.

'You ought to understand how any copper would feel about a cover-up like this,' he said. 'You'll have to make statements of all of it – at least for the files. I think it may be possible to keep the two killings separate and to keep General Sternwood's name out of both of them. Do you know why I'm not tearing your ear off?'

'No. I expected to get both ears torn off.'

'What are you getting for it all?'

'Twenty-five dollars a day and expenses.'

'That would make fifty dollars and a little gasolene so far.'

'About that.'

He put his head on one side and rubbed the back of his left little finger along the lower edge of his chin.

'And for that amount of money you're willing to get yourself in Dutch with half the law enforcement of this country?'

'I don't like it,' I said. 'But what the hell am I to do? I'm on a case. I'm selling what I have to sell to make a living. What little guts and intelligence the Lord gave me and a willingness to get pushed around in order to protect a client. It's against my principles to tell as much as I've told to-night, without consulting the General. As for the cover-up, I've been in police business myself, as you know. They come a dime a dozen in any big city. Cops get very large and emphatic when an outsider tries to hide anything, but they do the same things themselves every other day, to oblige their friends or anybody with a little pull. And I'm not through. I'm still on the case. I'd do the same thing again, if I had to.'

'Providing Cronjager doesn't get your licence,' Wilde grinned. 'You said you held back a couple of personal matters. Of what import?'

'I'm still on the case,' I said, and stared straight into his eyes.

Wilde smiled at me. He had the frank daring smile of an Irishman. 'Let me tell you something, son. My father was a close friend of old Sternwood. I've done all my office permits – and maybe a good deal more – to save the old man from grief. But in the long run it can't be done. Those girls of his are bound certain to hook up with something that can't be hushed, especially that little blonde brat. They ought not to be running around loose. I blame the old man for that. I guess he doesn't realize what the world is to-day. And there's another thing I might mention while we're talking man to man and I don't have to growl at you. I'll bet a dollar to a Canadian dime that the General's afraid his son-in-law, the ex-bootlegger, is mixed up in this somewhere, and what he really hoped you would find out is that he isn't. What do you think of that?'

'Regan didn't sound like a blackmailer, what I heard of him. He had a soft spot where he was and he walked out on it.'

Wilde snorted. 'The softness of that spot neither you nor I could judge. If he was a certain sort of man, it would not have been so very soft. Did the General tell you he was looking for Regan?'

'He told me he wished he knew where he was and that he was all right. He liked Regan and was hurt the way he bounced off without telling the old man good-bye.'

Wilde leaned back and frowned. 'I see,' he said in a changed voice. His hand moved the stuff on his desk around, laid Geiger's blue notebook to one side and pushed the other exhibits towards me. 'You may as well take these,' he said. 'I've no further use for them.'

19

It was close to eleven when I put my car away and walked around to the front of the Hobart Arms. The plate-glass door was put on the lock at ten, so I had to get my keys out. Inside, in the square barren lobby, a man put a green evening paper down beside a potted palm and flicked a cigarette butt into the tub the palm grew in. He stood up and waved his hat at me and said: 'The boss wants to talk to you. You sure keep your friends waiting, pal.'

I stood still and looked at his flattened nose and club steak ear.

'What about?'

'What do you care? Just keep your nose clean and everything will be jake.' His hand hovered near the upper button-hole of his open coat.

'I smell of policemen,' I said. 'I'm too tired to talk, too tired to eat, too tired to think. But if you think I'm not too tired to take orders from Eddie Mars – try getting your gat out before I shoot your good ear off.'

'Nuts. You ain't got no gun.' He stared at me levelly. His dark wiry brows closed in together and his mouth made a downward curve.

'That was then,' I told him. 'I'm not always naked.'

He waved his left hand. 'Okey. You win. I wasn't told to blast anybody. You'll hear from him.'

'Too late will be too soon,' I said, and turned slowly as he passed me on his way to the door. He opened it and went out without looking back. I grinned at my own foolishness, went along to the elevator and upstairs to the apartment. I took Carmen's little gun out of my pocket and laughed at it. Then I cleaned it thoroughly, oiled it, wrapped it in a piece of canton flannel and locked it up. I made myself a drink and was drinking it when the phone rang. I sat down beside the table on which it stood.

'So you're tough to-night,' Eddie Mars's voice said.

'Big, fast, tough and full of prickles. What can I do for you?'

'Cops over there – you know where. You keep me out of it?'

'Why should I?'

'I'm nice to be nice to, soldier. I'm not nice not to be nice to.'

'Listen hard and you'll hear my teeth chattering.'

He laughed dryly. 'Did you – or did you?'

'I did. I'm damned if I know why. I guess it was just complicated enough without you.'

'Thanks, soldier. Who gunned him?'

'Read it in the paper to-morrow – maybe.'

'I want to know now.'

'Do you get everything you want?'

'No. Is that an answer, soldier?'

'Somebody you never heard of gunned him. Let it go at that.'

'If that's on the level, some day I may be able to do you a favour.'

'Hang up and let me go to bed.'

He laughed again. 'You're looking for Rusty Regan, aren't you?'

'A lot of people seem to think I am, but I'm not.'

'If you were, I could give you an idea. Drop in and see me down at the beach. Any time. Glad to see you.'

'Maybe.'

'Be seeing you then.' The phone clicked and I sat holding it with a savage patience. Then I dialled the Sternwoods' number and heard it ring four or five times and then the butler's suave voice saying: 'General Sternwood's residence.'

'This is Marlowe. Remember me? I met you about a hundred years ago – or was it yesterday?'

'Yes, Mr Marlowe. I remember, of course.'

'Is Mrs Regan home?'

'Yes, I believe so. Would you –'

I cut in on him with a sudden change of mind. 'No. You give her the message. Tell her I have the pictures, all of them, and that everything is all right.'

'Yes . . . yes . . .' The voice seemed to shake a little. 'You have the pictures – all of them – and everything is all right . . . Yes, sir. I may say – thank you very much, sir.'

The phone rang back in five minutes. I had finished my drink and it made me feel as if I could eat the dinner

I had forgotten all about; I went out leaving the telephone ringing. It was ringing when I came back. It rang at intervals until half-past twelve. At that time I put my lights out and opened the windows up and muffled the phone bell with a piece of paper and went to bed. I had a bellyful of the Sternwood family.

I read all three of the morning papers over my eggs and bacon the next morning. Their accounts of the affair came as close to the truth as newspaper stories usually come – as close as Mars is to Saturn. None of the three connected Owen Taylor, driver of the Lido Pier Suicide Car, with the Laurel Canyon Exotic Bungalow Slaying. None of them mentioned the Sternwoods, Bernie Ohls or me. Owen Taylor was 'chauffeur to a wealthy family'. Captain Cronjager of the Hollywood Division got all the credit for solving the two slayings in his district, which were supposed to arise out of a dispute over the proceeds from a wire service maintained by one Geiger in the back of the bookstore on Hollywood Boulevard. Brody had shot Geiger and Carol Lundgren had shot Brody in revenge. Police were holding Carol Lundgren in custody. He had confessed. He had a bad record – probably in high school. Police were also holding one Agnes Lozelle, Geiger's secretary, as a material witness.

It was a nice write-up. It gave the impression that Geiger had been killed the night before, that Brody had been killed about an hour later, and that Captain Cronjager had solved both murders while lighting a cigarette. The suicide of Taylor made Page One of Section II. There was a photo of the sedan on the deck of the power lighter, with the licence plate blacked out, and something covered with a cloth lying on the deck beside the running board. Owen Taylor had been despondent and in poor health. His family lived in Dubuque, and his body would be shipped there. There would be no inquest.

20

Captain Gregory of the Missing Persons Bureau laid my card down on his wide flat desk and arranged it so that its edges exactly paralleled the edges of the desk. He studied it with his head on one side, grunted, swung around in his swivel chair and looked out of his window at the barred top floor of the Hall of Justice half a block away. He was a burly man with tired eyes and the slow deliberate movements of a night watchman. His voice was toneless, flat and uninterested.

'Private dick, eh?' he said, not looking at me at all, but looking out of his window. Smoke wisped from the blackened bowl of a briar that hung on his eye tooth. 'What can I do for you?'

'I'm working for General Guy Sternwood, 3765 Alta Brea Crescent, West Hollywood.'

Captain Gregory blew a little smoke from the corner of his mouth without removing the pipe. 'On what?'

'Not exactly on what you're working on, but I'm interested. I thought you could help me.'

'Help you on what?'

'General Sternwood's a rich man,' I said. 'He's an old

friend of the DA's father. If he wants to hire a full-time boy to run errands for him, that's no reflection on the police. It's just a luxury he is able to afford himself.'

'What makes you think I'm doing anything for him?'

I didn't answer that. He swung round slowly and heavily in his swivel chair and put his large feet flat on the bare linoleum that covered his floor. His office had the musty smell of years of routine. He stared at me bleakly.

'I don't want to waste your time, Captain,' I said and pushed my chair back – about four inches.

He didn't move. He kept on staring at me out of his washed-out tired eyes. 'You know the DA?'

'I've met him. I worked for him once. I know Bernie Ohls, his chief investigator, pretty well.'

Captain Gregory reached for a phone and mumbled into it: 'Get me Ohls at the DA's office.'

He sat holding the phone down on its cradle. Moments passed. Smoke drifted from his pipe. His eyes were heavy and motionless like his hand. The bell tinkled and he reached for my card with his left hand. 'Ohls? . . . Al Gregory at headquarters. A guy named Philip Marlowe is in my office. His card says he's a private investigator. He wants information from me . . . Yeah? What does he look like? . . . Okey, thanks.'

He dropped the phone and took his pipe out of his mouth and tamped the tobacco with the brass cap of a heavy pencil. He did it carefully and solemnly, as if that was as important as anything he would have to do that day. He leaned back and stared at me some more.

'What you want?'

'An idea of what progress you're making, if any.'

He thought that over. 'Regan?' he asked finally.

'Sure.'

'Know him?'

'I never saw him. I hear he's a good-looking Irishman in his late thirties, that he was once in the liquor racket, that he married General Sternwood's older daughter and that they didn't click. I'm told he disappeared about a month back.'

'Sternwood oughta think himself lucky instead of hiring private talent to beat around in the tall grass.'

'The General took a big fancy to him. Such things happen. The old man is crippled and lonely. Regan used to sit around with him and keep him company.'

'What you think you can do that we can't do?'

'Nothing at all, in so far as finding Regan goes. But there's a rather mysterious blackmail angle. I want to make sure Regan isn't involved. Knowing where he is or isn't might help.'

'Brother, I'd like to help you, but I don't know where he is. He pulled down the curtain and that's that.'

'Pretty hard to do against your organization, isn't it, Captain?'

'Yeah – but it can be done – for a while.' He touched a bell button on the side of his desk. A middle-aged woman put her head in at a side door. 'Get me the file on Terence Regan, Abba.'

The door closed. Captain Gregory and I looked at each other in some more heavy silence. The door opened again and the woman put a tabbed green file on his desk. Captain

Gregory nodded her out, put a pair of heavy horn-rimmed glasses on his veined nose and turned the papers in the file over slowly. I rolled a cigarette around in my fingers.

'He blew on the 16th of September,' he said. 'The only thing important about that is it was the chauffeur's day off and nobody saw Regan take his car out. It was late afternoon, though. We found the car four days later in a garage belonging to a ritzy bungalow court place near the Sunset Towers. A garage man reported it to the stolen car detail, said it didn't belong there. The place is called the Casa de Oro. There's an angle to that I'll tell you about in a minute. We couldn't find out anything about who put the car in there. We print the car but don't find any prints that are on the file anywhere. The car in that garage don't jibe with foul play, although there's a reason to suspect foul play. It jibes with something else I'll tell you about in a minute.'

I said: 'That jibes with Eddie Mars's wife being on the missing list.'

He looked annoyed. 'Yeah. We investigate the tenants and find she's living there. Left about the time Regan did, within two days anyway. A guy who sounds a bit like Regan had been seen with her, but we don't get a positive identification. It's goddamned funny in this police racket how an old woman can look out of a window and see a guy running and pick him out of a line-up six months later, but we can show hotel help a clear photo and they just can't be sure.'

'That's one of the qualifications for good hotel help,' I said.

'Yeah. Eddie Mars and his wife didn't live together, but they were friendly, Eddie says. Here's some of the possibilities. First off Regan carried fifteen grand, packed it in his clothes all the time. Real money, they tell me. Not just a top card and a bunch of hay. That's a lot of jack but this Regan might be the boy to have it around so he could take it out and look at it when somebody was looking at him. Then again maybe he wouldn't give a damn. His wife says he never made a nickel off old man Sternwood except room and board and a Packard 120 his wife gave him. Tie that for an ex-legger in the rich gravy.'

'It beats me,' I said.

'Well, here we are with a guy who ducks out and has fifteen grand in his pants and folks know it. Well, that's money. I might duck out myself, if I had fifteen grand, and me with two kids in high school. So the first thought is somebody rolls him for it and rolls him too hard, so they have to take him out in the desert and plant him among the cactuses. But I don't like that too well. Regan carried a gat and had plenty of experience using it, and not just in a greasy-faced liquor mob. I understand he commanded a whole brigade in the Irish troubles back in 1922 or whenever it was. A guy like that wouldn't be white meat to a heister. Then, his car being in that garage makes whoever rolled him know he was sweet on Eddie Mars's wife, which he was, I guess, but it ain't something every poolroom bum would know.'

'Got a photo?' I asked.

'Him, not her. That's funny too. There's a lot of funny angles to this case. Here.' He pushed a shiny print across the desk and I looked at an Irish face that was more sad than merry and more reserved than brash. Not the face of a tough guy and not the face of a man who could be pushed around much by anybody. Straight dark brows with strong bone under them. A forehead wide rather than high, a mat of dark clustering hair, a thin short nose, a wide mouth. A chin that had strong lines but was small for the mouth. A face that looked a little taut, the face of a man who would move fast and play for keeps. I passed the print back. I would know that face, if I saw it.

Captain Gregory knocked his pipe out and refilled it and tamped the tobacco down with his thumb. He lit it, blew smoke and began to talk again.

'Well, there could be people who would know he was sweet on Eddie Mars's frau. Besides Eddie himself. For a wonder *he* knew it. But he don't seem to give a damn. We check him pretty thoroughly around that time. Of course Eddie wouldn't have knocked him off out of jealousy. The set-up would point to him too obvious.'

'It depends how smart he is,' I said. 'He might try the double bluff.'

Captain Gregory shook his head. 'If he's smart enough to get by in his racket, he's too smart for that. I get your idea. He pulls the dumb act because he thinks we wouldn't expect him to pull the dumb play. From a police angle that's wrong. Because he'd have us in his hair so much it would interfere with his business. *You* might think a dumb play would be smart. I might think so. The rank and file wouldn't. They'd make his life miserable. I've ruled it out. If I'm wrong, you can prove it on me and I'll eat my chair cushion. Till then I'm leaving Eddie in the clear. Jealousy is a bad motive for his type. Top-flight racketeers have business brains. They learn to do things that are good policy and let their personal feelings take care of themselves. I'm leaving that out.'

'What are you leaving in?'

'The dame and Regan himself. Nobody else. She was a blonde then, but she won't be now. We don't find her car, so they probably left in it. They had a long start on us – fourteen days. Except for that car of Regan's I don't figure we'd have got the case at all. Of course I'm used to them that way, especially in good-class families. And of course everything I've done has had to be under the hat.'

He leaned back and thumped the arms of his chair with the heels of his large heavy hands.

'I don't see nothing to do but wait,' he said. 'We've got readers out, but it's too soon to look for results. Regan had fifteen grand we know of. The girl had some, maybe a lot in rocks. But they'll run out of dough some day. Regan will cash a cheque, drop a marker, write a letter. They're in a strange town and they've got new names, but they've got the same old appetites. They got to get back in the fiscal system.'

'What did the girl do before she married Eddie Mars?'

'Torcher.'

'Can't you get any old professional photos?'

'No. Eddie must have had some, but he won't loosen up. He wants her let alone. I can't make him. He's got friends in town, or he wouldn't be what he is.' He grunted. 'Any of this do you any good?'

I said: 'You'll never find either of them. The Pacific Ocean is too close.'

'What I said about my chair cushion still goes. We'll find him. It may take time. It could take a year or two.'

'General Sternwood may not live that long,' I said.

'We've done all we could, brother. If he wants to put out a reward and spend some money, we might get results. The city don't give me the kind of money it takes.' His large eyes peered at me and his scratchy eyebrows moved. 'You serious about thinking Eddie put them both down?'

I laughed. 'No. I was just kidding. I think what you think, Captain. That Regan ran away with a woman who meant more to him than a rich wife he didn't get along with. Besides, she isn't rich yet.'

'You met her, I suppose?'

'Yes. She'd make a jazzy weekend, but she'd be wearing for a steady diet.'

He grunted and I thanked him for his time and information and left. A grey Plymouth sedan tailed me away from the City Hall. I gave it a chance to catch up with me on a quiet street. It refused the offer, so I shook it off and went about my business.

21

I didn't go near the Sternwood family. I went back to the office and sat in my swivel chair and tried to catch up on my foot-dangling. There was a gusty wind blowing in at the windows and the soot from the oil burners of the hotel next door was down-draughted into the room and rolling across the top of the desk like tumbleweed drifting across a vacant lot. I was thinking about going out to lunch and that life was pretty flat and that it would probably be just as flat if I took a drink and that taking a drink all alone at that time of day wouldn't be any fun anyway. I was thinking this when Norris called up. In his carefully polite manner he said that General Sternwood was not feeling very well and that certain items in the newspaper had been read to him and he assumed that my investigation was now completed.

'Yes, as regards Geiger,' I said. 'I didn't shoot him, you know.'

'The General didn't suppose you did, Mr Marlowe.'

'Does the General know anything about those photographs Mrs Regan was worrying about?'

'No, sir. Decidedly not.'

'Did you know what the General gave me?'

'Yes, sir. Three notes and a card, I believe.'

'Right. I'll return them. As to the photos I think I'd better just destroy them.'

'Very good, sir. Mrs Regan tried to reach you a number of times last night – '

'I was out getting drunk,' I said.

'Yes. Very necessary, sir, I'm sure. The General has instructed me to send you a cheque for five hundred dollars. Will that be satisfactory?'

'More than generous,' I said.

'And I presume we may now consider the incident closed?'

'Oh, sure. Tight as a vault with a busted time lock.'

'Thank you, sir. I am sure we all appreciate it. When the General is feeling a little better – possibly tomorrow – he would like to thank you in person.'

'Fine,' I said. 'I'll come out and drink some more of his brandy, maybe with champagne.'

'I shall see that some is properly iced,' the old boy said, almost with a smirk in his voice.

That was that. We said good-bye and hung up. The coffee shop smell from next door came in at the windows with the soot but failed to make me hungry. So I got out my office bottle and took the drink and let my self-respect ride its own race.

I counted it up on my fingers. Rusty Regan had run away from a lot of money and a handsome wife to go wandering with a vague blonde who was more or less married to a racketeer named Eddie Mars. He had gone suddenly without good-byes and there might be any number of reasons for that. The General had been too proud, or, at the first interview he gave me, too careful, to tell me the Missing Persons Bureau had the matter in hand. The Missing Persons people were dead on their feet on it and evidently didn't think it worth bothering over. Regan had done what he had done and that was his business. I agreed with Captain Gregory that Eddie Mars would have been very unlikely to involve himself in a double murder just because another man had gone to town with the blonde he was not even living with. It might have annoyed him, but business is business, and you have to hold your teeth clamped around Hollywood to keep from chewing on stray blondes. If there had been a lot of money involved, that would be different. But fifteen grand wouldn't be a lot of money to Eddie Mars. He was no two-bit chiseller like Brody.

Geiger was dead and Carmen would have to find some other shady character to drink exotic blends of hooch with. I didn't suppose she would have any trouble. All she would have to do would be to stand on the corner for five minutes and look coy. I hoped that the next grifter who dropped the hook on her would play her a little more smoothly, a little more for the long haul rather than the quick touch.

Mrs Regan knew Eddie Mars well enough to borrow money from him. That was natural, if she played roulette and was a good loser. Any gambling house owner would lend a good client money in a pinch. Apart from this they had an added bond of interest in Regan. He was her husband and he had gone off with Eddie Mars's wife.

Carol Lundgren, the boy killer with the limited vocabulary, was out of circulation for a long, long time, even if they didn't strap him in a chair over a bucket of acid. They wouldn't, because he would take a plea and save the country money. They all do when they don't have the price of a big lawyer. Agnes Lozelle was in custody as a material witness. They wouldn't need her for that, if Carol took a plea, and if he pleaded guilty on arraignment, they would turn her loose. They wouldn't want to open up any angles on Geiger's business, apart from which they had nothing on her.

That left me. I had concealed a murder and suppressed evidence for twenty-four hours, but I was still at large and had a five-hundred-dollar cheque coming. The smart thing for me to do was to take another drink and forget the whole mess.

That being the obviously smart thing to do, I called Eddie Mars and told him I was coming down to Las Olindas that evening to talk to him. That was how smart I was.

I got down there about nine, under a hard high October moon that lost itself in the top layers of a beach fog. The Cypress Club was at the far end of the town, a rambling frame mansion that had once been the summer residence of a rich man named De Cazens, and later had been a hotel. It was now a big dark outwardly shabby place in a thick grove of wind-twisted Monterey cypresses, which gave it its name. It had enormous scrolled porches, turrets all over the place, stained-glass trims around the big windows, big empty stables at the back, a general air of nostalgic decay. Eddie Mars had left the outside much as he had found it, instead of making it over to look like an MGM set. I left my car on a street with sputtering arc lights and walked into the grounds along a damp gravel path to the main entrance. A doorman in a double-breasted guards coat let me into a huge dim silent lobby from which a white oak staircase curved majestically up to the darkness of an upper floor. I checked my hat and coat and waited, listening to music and confused voices behind heavy double doors. They seemed a long way off, and not quite of the same world as the building itself. Then the slim pasty-faced blonde man who had been with Eddie Mars and the pug at Geiger's place came through a door under the staircase, smiled at me bleakly and took me back with him along a carpeted hall to the boss's office.

This was a square room with a deep old bay window and a stone fireplace in which a fire of juniper logs burned lazily. It was wainscoted in walnut and had a frieze of faded damask above the panelling. The ceiling was high and remote. There was a smell of cold sea.

Eddie Mars's dark sheenless desk didn't belong in the room, but neither did anything made after 1900. His carpet had a Florida suntan. There was a bartop radio in the corner and a Sèvres china tea set on a copper tray beside a samovar. I wondered who that was for. There was a door in the corner that had a time lock on it.

Eddie Mars grinned at me sociably and shook hands and moved his chin at the vault. 'I'm a pushover for a heist mob here except for that thing,' he said cheerfully. 'The local johns drop in every morning and watch me open it. I have an arrangement with them.'

'You hinted you had something for me,' I said. 'What is it?'

'What's your hurry? Have a drink and sit down.'

'No hurry at all. You and I haven't anything to talk about but business.'

'You'll have the drink and like it,' he said. He mixed a couple and put mine down beside a red leather chair and stood crosslegged against the desk himself, one hand in the side pocket of his midnight-blue dinner jacket, the thumb outside and the nail glistening. In dinner clothes he looked a little harder than in grey flannel, but he still looked like a horseman. We drank and nodded at each other.

'Ever been here before?' he asked.

'During prohibition. I don't get any kick out of gambling.'

'Not with money,' he smiled. 'You ought to look in tonight. One of your friends is outside betting the wheels. I hear she's doing pretty well. Vivian Regan.'

I sipped my drink and took one of his monogrammed cigarettes.

'I kind of liked the way you handled that yesterday,' he said. 'You made me sore at the time but I could see afterwards how right you were. You and I ought to get along. How much do I owe you?'

'For doing what?'

'Still careful, eh? I have my pipeline into headquarters, or I wouldn't be here. I get them the way they happen, not the way you read them in the papers.' He showed me his large white teeth.

'How much have you got?' I asked.

'You're not talking money?'

'Information was the way I understood it.'

'Information about what?'

'You have a short memory. Regan.'

'Oh, that.' He waved his glistening nails in the quiet light from one of those bronze lamps that shoot a beam at the ceiling. 'I hear you got the information already. I felt I owed you a fee. I'm used to paying for nice treatment.'

'I didn't drive down here to make a touch. I get paid for what I do. Not much by your standards, but I make out. One customer at a time is a good rule. You didn't bump Regan off, did you?'

'No. Did you think I did?'

'I wouldn't put it past you.'

He laughed. 'You're kidding.'

I laughed. 'Sure, I'm kidding. I never saw Regan, but I saw his photo. You haven't got men for the work. And while we're on that subject don't send me any more gun punks with orders. I might get hysterical and blow one down.'

He looked through his glass at the fire, set it down on the end of the desk and wiped his lips with a sheer lawn handkerchief.

'You talk a good game,' he said. 'But I dare say you can break a hundred and ten. You're not really interested in Regan are you?'

'No, not professionally. I haven't been asked to be. But

I know somebody who would like to know where he is.'

'She doesn't give a damn,' he said.

'I mean her father.'

He wiped his lips again and looked at the handkerchief almost as if he expected to find blood on it. He drew his thick grey eyebrows close together and fingered the side of his weatherbeaten nose.

'Geiger was trying to blackmail the General,' I said. 'The General wouldn't say so, but I figure he was at least half scared Regan might be behind it.'

Eddie Mars laughed. 'Uh-uh. Geiger worked that one on everybody. It was strictly his own idea. He'd get notes from people that looked legal – were legal, I dare say, except that he wouldn't have dared sue on them. He'd present notes, with a nice flourish, leaving himself empty-handed. If he drew an ace, he had a prospect that scared and he went to work. If he didn't draw an ace, he just dropped the whole thing.'

'Clever guy,' I said. 'He dropped it all right. Dropped it and fell on it. How come *you* know all this?'

He shrugged impatiently. 'I wish to Christ I didn't know half the stuff that's brought to me. Knowing other people's business is the worst investment a man can make in my circle. Then if it was just Geiger you were after, you're washed up on that angle.'

'Washed up and paid off.'

'I'm sorry about that. I wish old Sternwood would hire himself a soldier like you on a straight salary, to keep those girls of his home at least a few nights a week.'

'Why?'

His mouth looked sulky. 'They're plain trouble. Take the dark one. She's a pain in the neck around here. If she loses, she plunges and I end up with a fistful of paper which nobody will discount at any price. She has no money of her own except an allowance and what's in the old man's will is a secret. If she wins, she takes my money home with her.'

'You get it back the next night,' I said.

'I get some of it back. But over a period of time I'm loser.'

He looked earnestly at me, as if that was important to me. I wondered why he thought it necessary to tell me at all. I yawned and finished my drink.

'I'm going out and look the joint over,' I said.

'Yes, do.' He pointed to a door near the vault door. 'That leads to a door behind the tables.'

'I'd rather go in the way the suckers enter.'

'Okey. As you please. We're friends, aren't we, soldier?'

'Sure.' I stood up and we shook hands.

'Maybe I can do you a real favour some day,' he said. 'You got it all from Gregory this time.'

'So you own a piece of him too.'

'Oh not that bad. We're just friends.'

I stared at him for a moment, then went over to the door I had come in at. I looked back at him when I had it open.

'You don't have anybody tailing me around in a grey Plymouth sedan, do you?'

His eyes widened sharply. He looked jarred. 'Hell, no. Why should I?'

'I couldn't imagine,' I said, and went on out. I thought his surprise looked genuine enough to be believed. I thought he even looked a little worried. I couldn't think of any reason for that.

22

It was about ten-thirty when the little yellow-sashed Mexican orchestra got tired of playing a low-voiced prettied-up rhumba that nobody was dancing to. The gourd player rubbed his finger tips together as if they were sore and got a cigarette into his mouth almost with the same movement. The other four, with a timed simultaneous stoop, reached under their chairs for glasses from which they sipped, smacking their lips and flashing their eyes. Tequila, their manner said. It was probably mineral water. The pretence was as wasted as the music. Nobody was looking at them.

The room had been a ballroom once and Eddie Mars had changed it only as much as his business compelled him. No chromium glitter, no indirect lighting from behind angular cornices, no fused glass pictures, or chairs in violent leather and polished metal tubing, none of the pseudo-modernistic circus of the typical Hollywood night trap. The light was from heavy crystal chandeliers and the rose-damask panels of the wall were still the same rose damask, a little faded by time and darkened by dust, that had been matched long ago against the parquetry floor, of which only a small glass-smooth space in front of the little Mexican orchestra showed bare. The rest was covered by a heavy old-rose carpeting that must have cost plenty. The parquetry was made of a dozen kinds of hardwood, from Burma teak through half a dozen shades of oak and ruddy wood that looked like mahogany, and fading out to the hard pale wild lilac of the California hills, all laid in elaborate patterns, with the accuracy of a transit.

It was still a beautiful room and now there was roulette in it instead of measured, old-fashioned dancing. There were three tables close to the far wall. A low bronze railing joined them and made a fence around the croupiers. All three tables were working, but the crowd was at the middle one. I could see Vivian Regan's black head close to it, from across the room where I was leaning against the bar and turning a small glass of bacardi around on the mahogany.

The bartender leaned beside me watching the cluster of well-dressed people at the middle table. 'She's pickin' 'em to-night, right on the nose,' he said. 'That tall black-headed frail.'

'Who is she?'

'I wouldn't know her name. She comes here a lot though.'

'The hell you wouldn't know her name.'

'I just work here, mister,' he said without any animosity. 'She's all alone too. The guy was with her passed out. They took him out to his car.'

'I'll take her home,' I said.

'The hell you will. Well, I wish you luck anyways.

Should I gentle up that bacardi or do you like it the way it is?'

'I like it the way it is as well as I like it at all,' I said.

'Me, I'd just as leave drink croup medicine,' he said.

The crowd parted and two men in evening clothes pushed their way out and I saw the back of her neck and her bare shoulders in the opening. She wore a low-cut dress of dull green velvet. It looked too dressy for the occasion. The crowd closed and hid all but her black head. The two men came across the room and leaned against the bar and asked for Scotch and soda. One of them was flushed and excited. He was mopping his face with a black-bordered handkerchief. The double satin stripes down the side of his trousers were wide enough for tyre tracks.

'Boy, I never saw such a run,' he said in a jittery voice. 'Eight wins and two stand-offs in a row on that red. That's roulette, boy, that's roulette.'

'It gives me the itch,' the other one said. 'She's betting a grand at a crack. She can't lose.' They put their beaks in their drinks, gurgled swiftly and went back.

'So wise the little men are,' the barkeeper said. 'A grand a crack, huh. I saw an old horseface in Havana once –'

The noise swelled over at the middle table and a chiselled foreign voice rose above it saying: 'If you will just be patient a moment, madam. The table cannot cover your bet. Mr Mars will be here in a moment.'

I left my bacardi and padded across the carpet. The little orchestra started to play a tango, rather loud. No one was dancing or intending to dance. I moved through a scattering of people in dinner clothes and full evening dress and sports clothes and business suits to the end table at the left. It had gone dead. Two croupiers stood behind it with their heads together and their eyes sideways. One moved a rake back and forth aimlessly over the empty layout. They were both staring at Vivian Regan.

Her long lashes twitched and her face looked unnaturally white. She was at the middle table, exactly opposite the wheel. There was a disordered pile of money and chips in front of her. It looked like a lot of money. She spoke to the croupier with a cool, insolent, ill-tempered drawl.

'What kind of a cheap outfit is this, I'd like to know. Get busy and spin that wheel, highpockets. I want one more play and I'm playing table stakes. You take it away fast enough I've noticed, but when it comes to dishing it out you start to whine.'

The croupier smiled a cold polite smile that had looked at thousands of boors and millions of fools. His tall dark disinterested manner was flawless. He said gravely: 'The table cannot cover your bet, madam. You have over sixteen thousand dollars there.'

'It's your money,' the girl jeered. 'Don't you want it back?'

A man beside her tried to tell her something. She turned swiftly and spat something at him and he faded back into the crowd red-faced. A door opened in the panelling at the far end of the enclosed place made by the bronze railing. Eddie Mars came through the door with a set indifferent smile on his face, his hands thrust into the pockets of his dinner jacket, both thumbnails glistening outside. He seemed to like that pose. He strolled behind the croupiers and stopped at the corner of the middle table. He spoke with lazy calm, less politely than the croupier.

'Something the matter, Mrs Regan?'

She turned her face to him with a sort of lunge. I saw the curve of her cheek stiffen, as if with an almost unbearable inner tautness. She didn't answer him.

Eddie Mars said gravely: 'If you're not playing any more, you must let me send someone home with you.'

The girl flushed. Her cheekbones stood out white in her face. Then she laughed off-key. She said bitterly:

'One more play, Eddie. Everything I have on the red. I like red. It's the colour of blood.'

Eddie Mars smiled faintly, then nodded and reached into his inner breast pocket. He drew out a large pin-seal wallet with gold corners and tossed it carelessly along the table to the croupier. 'Cover her bet in even thousands,' he said, 'if no one objects to this turn of the wheel being just for the lady.'

No one objected. Vivian Regan leaned down and pushed all her winnings savagely with both hands on to the large red diamond on the layout.

The croupier leaned over the table without haste. He counted and stacked her money and chips, placed all but a few chips and bills in a neat pile and pushed the rest back off the layout with his rake. He opened Eddie Mars's wallet and drew out two flat packets of thousand-dollar bills. He broke one, counted six bills out, added them to the unbroken packet, put the four loose bills in the wallet and laid it aside as carelessly as if it had been a packet of matches. Eddie Mars didn't touch the wallet. Nobody moved except the croupier. He spun the wheel lefthanded and sent the ivory ball skittering along the upper edge with a casual flirt of his wrist. Then he drew his hands back and folded his arms.

Vivian's lips parted slowly until her teeth caught the light and glittered like knives. The ball drifted lazily down the slope of the wheel and bounced on the chromium ridges above the numbers. After a long time and then very suddenly motion left it with a dry click. The wheel slowed, carrying the ball around with it. The croupier didn't unfold his arms until the wheel had entirely ceased to revolve.

'The red wins,' he said formally, without interest. The little ivory ball lay in Red 25, the third number from the Double Zero. Vivian Regan put her head back and laughed triumphantly.

The croupier lifted his rake and slowly pushed the stack of thousand-dollar bills across the layout, added them to the stake, pushed everything slowly out of the field of play.

Eddie Mars smiled, put his wallet back in his pocket, turned on his heel and left the room through the door in the panelling.

A dozen people let their breath out at the same time and broke for the bar. I broke with them and got to the far end of the room before Vivian had gathered up her winnings and turned away from the table. I went out into the large quiet lobby, got my hat and coat from the check girl, dropped a quarter in her tray and went out on the porch. The doorman loomed up beside me and said: 'Can I get your car for you, sir?'

I said: 'I'm just going for a walk.'

The scrollwork along the edge of the porch roof was wet with the fog. The fog dripped from the Monterey cypresses that shadowed off into nothing towards the cliff above the ocean. You could see a scant dozen feet in any direction. I went down the porch steps and drifted off through the trees, following an indistinct path until I could hear the wash of the surf licking at the fog, low down at the bottom of the cliff. There wasn't a gleam of light anywhere. I could see a dozen trees clearly at one time, another dozen dimly, then nothing at all but the fog. I circled to the left and drifted back towards the gravel path that went around to the stables where they parked the cars. When I could make out the outlines of the house I stopped. A little in front of me I had heard a man cough.

My steps hadn't made any sound on the soft moist turf. The man coughed again, then stifled the cough with a handkerchief or a sleeve. While he was still doing that I moved forward closer to him. I made him out, a vague shadow close to the path. Something made me step behind a tree and crouch down. The man turned his head. His face should have been a white blur when he did that. It wasn't. It remained dark. There was a mask over it.

I waited, behind the tree.

23

Light steps, the steps of a woman, came along the invisible pathway and the man in front of me moved forward and seemed to lean against the fog. I couldn't see the woman, then I could see her indistinctly. The arrogant carriage of her head seemed familiar. The man stepped out very quickly. The two figures blended in the fog, seemed to be part of the fog. There was dead silence for a moment. The man said:

'This is a gun, lady. Gentle now. Sound carries in the fog. Just hand me the bag.'

The girl didn't make a sound. I moved forward a step. Quite suddenly I could see the foggy fuzz on the man's hat brim. The girl stood motionless. Then her breathing began to make a rasping sound, like a small file on soft wood.

'Yell,' the man said, 'and I'll cut you in half.'

She didn't yell. She didn't move. There was a movement from him, and a dry chuckle. 'It better be in here,' he said. A catch clicked and a fumbling sound came to me. The man turned and came towards my tree. When he had taken three or four steps he chuckled again. The chuckle was something out of my own memories. I reached a pipe out of my pocket and held it like a gun.

I called out softly: 'Hi, Lanny.'

The man stopped dead and started to bring his hand up. I said: 'No. I told you never to do that, Lanny. You're covered.'

Nothing moved. The girl back on the path didn't move. I didn't move. Lanny didn't move.

'Put the bag down between your feet, kid,' I told him. 'Slow and easy.'

He bent down. I jumped out and reached him still bent over. He straightened up against me breathing hard. His hands were empty.

'Tell me I can't get away with it,' I said. I leaned against him and took the gun out of his overcoat pocket. 'Somebody's always giving me guns,' I told him. 'I'm weighted down with them till I walk all crooked. Beat it.'

Our breaths met and mingled, our eyes were like the eyes of two tomcats on a wall. I stepped back.

'On your way, Lanny. No hard feelings. You keep it quiet and I keep it quiet. Okey?'

'Okey,' he said thickly.

The fog swallowed him. The faint sound of his steps and then nothing. I picked the bag up and felt in it and went towards the path. She still stood there motionless, a grey fur coat held tight around her throat with an ungloved hand on which a ring made a faint glitter. She wore no hat. Her dark parted hair was part of the darkness of the night. Her eyes too.

'Nice work, Marlowe. Are you my bodyguard now?' Her voice had a harsh note.

'Looks that way. Here's the bag.'

She took it. I said: 'Have you a car with you?'

She laughed. 'I came with a man. What are you doing here?'

'Eddie Mars wanted to see me.'

'I didn't know you knew him. Why?'

'I don't mind telling you. He thought I was looking for somebody he thought had run away with his wife.'

'Were you?'

'No.'

'Then what did you come for?'

'To find out why he thought I was looking for somebody he thought had run away with his wife.'

'Did you find out?'

'No.'

'You leak information like a radio announcer,' she said. 'I suppose it's none of my business – even if the man was my husband. I thought you weren't interested in that.'

'People keep throwing it at me.'

She clicked her teeth in annoyance. The incident of the masked man with the gun seemed to have made no impression on her at all. 'Well, take me to the garage,' she said. 'I have to look in at my escort.'

We walked along the path and around a corner of the building and there was light ahead, then around another corner and came to a bright enclosed stableyard lit with two floodlights. It was still paved with brick and still sloped down to a grating in the middle. Cars glistened and a man in a brown smock got up off a stool and came forward.

'Is my boy friend still blotto?' Vivian asked him carelessly.

'I'm afraid he is, miss. I put a rug over him and run the windows up. He's okey, I guess. Just kind of resting.'

We went over to a big Cadillac and the man in the smock pulled the rear door open. On the wide back seat, loosely arranged, covered to the chin with a plaid robe, a man lay snoring with his mouth open. He seemed to be a big blonde man who would hold a lot of liquor.

'Meet Mr Larry Cobb,' Vivian said. 'Mister Cobb – Mister Marlowe.'

I grunted.

'Mr Cobb was my escort,' she said. 'Such a nice escort, Mr Cobb. So attentive. You should see him sober. *I* should see him sober. Somebody should see him sober. I mean, just for the record. So it could become a part of history, that brief flashing moment, soon buried in time, but never forgotten – when Larry Cobb was sober.'

'Yeah,' I said.

'I've even thought of marrying him,' she went on in a high strained voice, as if the shock of the stick-up was just beginning to get to her. 'At odd times when nothing pleasant would come into my mind. We all have those spells. Lots of money, you know. A yacht, a place on Long Island, a place at Newport, a place at Bermuda, places dotted here and there all over the world probably – just a good Scotch bottle apart. And to Mr Cobb a bottle of Scotch is not very far.'

'Yeah,' I said. 'Does he have a driver to take him home?'

'Don't say "yeah". It's common.' She looked at me with arched eyebrows. The man in the smock was chewing his lower lip hard. 'Oh, undoubtedly a whole platoon of drivers. They probably do squads right in front of the garage every morning, buttons shining, harness gleaming, white gloves immaculate – a sort of West Point elegance about them.'

'Well, where the hell is this driver?' I asked.

'He drove hisself to-night,' the man in the smock said, almost apologetically. 'I could call his home and have somebody come down for him.'

Vivian turned around and smiled at him as if he had just presented her with a diamond tiara. 'That would be lovely,' she said. 'Would you do that? I really wouldn't want Mr Cobb to die like that – with his mouth open. Someone might think he had died of thirst.'

The man in the smock said: 'Not if they sniffed him, miss.'

She opened her bag and grabbed a handful of paper money and pushed it at him. 'You'll take care of him, I'm sure.'

'Jeeze,' the man said, pop-eyed. 'I sure will, miss.'

'Regan is the name,' she said sweetly. 'Mrs Regan. You'll probably see me again. Haven't been here long, have you?'

'No'm.' His hands were doing frantic things with the fistful of money he was holding.

'You'll get to love it here,' she said. She took hold of my arm. 'Let's ride in your car, Marlowe.'

'It's outside on the street.'

'Quite all right with me, Marlowe. I love a nice walk in the fog. You meet such interesting people.'

'Oh, nuts,' I said.

She held on to my arm and began to shake. She held me hard all the way to the car. She had stopped shaking by the time we reached it. I drove down a curving lane of trees on the blind side of the house. The lane opened on De Cazens Boulevard, the main drag of Las Olindas. We passed under the ancient sputtering arc lights and after a while there was a town, buildings, dead-looking stores, a service station with a light over a night bell, and at last a drugstore that was still open.

'You better have a drink,' I said.

She moved her chin, a point of paleness in the corner of the seat. I turned diagonally into the kerb and parked. 'A little black coffee and a smattering of rye would go well,' I said.

'I could get as drunk as two sailors and love it.'

I held the door for her and she got out close to me, brushing my cheek with her hair. We went into the drugstore. I bought a pint of rye at the liquor counter and carried it over to the stools and set it down on the cracked marble counter.

'Two coffees,' I said. 'Black, strong and made this year.'

'You can't drink liquor in here,' the clerk said. He had a washed-out blue smock, was thin on top as to hair, had fairly honest eyes and his chin would never hit a wall before he saw it.

Vivian Regan reached into her bag for a packet of cigarettes and shook a couple loose just like a man. She held them towards me.

'It's against the law to drink liquor in here,' the clerk said.

I lit the cigarettes and didn't pay any attention to him. He drew two cups of coffee from a tarnished nickel urn and set them in front of us. He looked at the bottle of rye, muttered under his breath and said wearily: 'Okey, I'll watch the street while you pour it.'

He went and stood at the display window with his back to us and his ears hanging out.

'My heart's in my mouth doing this,' I said, and unscrewed the top of the whisky bottle and loaded the coffee. 'The law enforcement in this town is terrific. All through prohibition Eddie Mars's place was a nightclub and they had two uniformed men in the lobby every night – to see that the guests didn't bring their own liquor instead of buying it from the house.'

The clerk turned suddenly and walked back behind the counter and went in behind the little glass window of the prescription room.

We sipped our loaded coffee. I looked at Vivian's face in the mirror back of the coffee urn. It was taut, pale, beautiful and wild. Her lips were red and harsh.

'You have wicked eyes,' I said. 'What's Eddie Mars got on you?'

She looked at me in the mirror. 'I took plenty away from him to-night at roulette – starting with five grand I borrowed from him yesterday and didn't have to use.'

'That might make him sore. You think he sent that loogan after you?'

'What's a loogan?'

'A guy with a gun.'

'Are you a loogan?'

'Sure,' I laughed. 'But strictly speaking a loogan is on the wrong side of the fence.'

'I often wonder if there is a wrong side.'

'We're losing the subject. What has Eddie Mars got on you?'

'You mean a hold on me of some sort?'

'Yes.'

Her lip curled. 'Wittier, please, Marlowe. Much wittier.'

'How's the General? I don't pretend to be witty.'

'Not too well. He didn't get up to-day. You could at least stop questioning me.'

'I remember a time when I thought the same about you. How much does the General know?'

'He probably knows everything.'

'Norris would tell him?'

'No. Wilde, the District Attorney, was out to see him. Did you burn those pictures?'

'Sure. You worry about your little sister, don't you – from time to time.'

'I think she's all I do worry about. I worry about Dad in a way, to keep things from him.'

'He hasn't many illusions,' I said, 'but I suppose he still has pride.'

'We're his blood. That's the hell of it.' She stared at

me in the mirror with deep, distant eyes. 'I don't want him to die despising his own blood. It was always wild blood, but it wasn't always rotten blood.'

'Is it now?'

'I guess you think so.'

'Not yours. You're just playing the part.'

She looked down. I sipped some more coffee and lit another cigarette for us. 'So you shoot people,' she said quietly. 'You're a killer.'

'Me? How?'

'The papers and the police fixed it up nicely. But I don't believe everything I read.'

'Oh, you think I accounted for Geiger – or Brody – or both of them.'

She didn't say anything. 'I didn't have to,' I said. 'I might have, I suppose, and got away with it. Neither of them would have hesitated to throw lead at me.'

'That makes you just a killer at heart, like all cops.'

'Oh, nuts.'

'One of those dark deadly quiet men who have no more feelings than a butcher has for slaughtered meat. I knew it the first time I saw you.'

'You've got enough shady friends to know different.'

'They're all soft compared to you.'

'Thanks, lady. You're no English muffin yourself.'

'Let's get out of this rotten little town.'

I paid the check, put the bottle of rye in my pocket, and we left. The clerk still didn't like me.

We drove away from Las Olindas through a series of little dank beach towns with shack-like houses built down on the sand close to the rumble of the surf and larger houses built back on the slopes behind. A yellow window shone here and there, but most of the houses were dark. A smell of kelp came in off the water and lay on the fog. The tyres sang on the moist concrete of the boulevard. The world was a wet emptiness.

We were close to Del Rey before she spoke to me for the first time since we left the drugstore. Her voice had a muffled sound, as if something was throbbing deep under it.

'Drive down by the Del Ray beach club. I want to look at the water. It's the next street on the left.'

There was a winking yellow light at the intersection. I turned the car and slid down a slope with a high bluff on one side, interurban tracks to the right, a low straggle of lights far off beyond the tracks, and then very far off a glitter of pier lights and a haze in the sky over a city. That way the fog was almost gone. The road crossed the tracks where they turned to run under the bluff, then reached a paved strip of waterfront highway that bordered an open and uncluttered beach. Cars were parked along the pavement, facing out to sea, dark. The lights of the beach club were a few hundred yards away.

I braked the car against the kerb and switched the headlights off and sat with my hands on the wheel. Under the thinning fog the surf curled and creamed, almost without sound, like a thought trying to form itself on the edge of consciousness.

'Move closer,' she said almost thickly.

I moved out from under the wheel into the middle of

the seat. She turned her body a little away from me as if to peer out of the window. Then she let herself fall backwards, without a sound, into my arms. Her head almost struck the wheel. Her eyes were closed, her face was dim. Then I saw that her eyes opened and flickered, the shine of them visible even in the darkness.

'Hold me close, you beast,' she said.

I put my arms around her loosely at first. Her hair had a harsh feeling against my face. I tightened my arms and lifted her up. I brought her face slowly up to my face. Her eyelids were flickering rapidly, like moth wings.

I kissed her tightly and quickly. Then a long slow clinging kiss. Her lips opened under mine. Her body began to shake in my arms.

'Killer,' she said softly, her breath going into my mouth.

I strained her against me until the shivering of her body was almost shaking mine. I kept on kissing her. After a long time she pulled her head away enough to say: 'Where do you live?'

'Hobart Arms. Franklin near Kenmore.'

'I've never seen it.'

'Want to?'

'Yes.'

'What has Eddie Mars got on you?'

Her body stiffened in my arms and her breath made a harsh sound. Her head pulled back until her eyes, wide open, ringed with white, were staring at me.

'So that's the way it is,' she said in a soft dull voice.

'That's the way it is. Kissing is nice, but your father didn't hire me to sleep with you.'

'You son of a bitch,' she said calmly, without moving.

I laughed in her face. 'Don't think I'm an icicle,' I said. 'I'm not blind or without senses. I have warm blood like the next guy. You're easy to take – too damned easy. What has Eddie Mars got on you?'

'If you say that again, I'll scream.'

'Go ahead and scream.'

She jerked away and pulled herself upright, far back in the corner of the car.

'Men have been shot for little things like that, Marlowe.'

'Men have been shot for practically nothing. The first time we met I told you I was a detective. Get it through your lovely head. I work at it, lady. I don't play at it.'

She fumbled in her bag and got a handkerchief out and bit on it, her head turned away from me. The tearing sound of the handkerchief came to me. She tore it with her teeth, slowly, time after time.

'What makes you think he has anything on me?' she whispered, her voice muffled by the handkerchief.

'He lets you win a lot of money and sends a gunpoke around to take it back for him. You're not more than mildly surprised. You didn't even thank me for saving it for you. I think the whole thing was just some kind of an act. If I wanted to flatter myself, I'd say it was at least partly for my benefit.'

'You think he can win or lose as he pleases.'

'Sure. On even money bets, four times out of five.'

'Do I have to tell you I loathe your guts, Mister Detective?'

'You don't owe me anything. I'm paid off.'

She tossed the shredded handkerchief out of the car window. 'You have a lovely way with women.'

'I like kissing you.'

'You kept your head beautifully. That's so flattering. Should I congratulate you, or my father?'

'I liked kissing you.'

Her voice became an icy drawl. 'Take me away from here, if you will be so kind. I'm quite sure I'd like to go home.'

'You won't be a sister to me?'

'If I had a razor, I'd cut your throat – just to see what ran out of it.'

'Caterpillar blood,' I said.

I started the car and turned it and drove back across the interurban tracks to the highway and so on into town and up to West Hollywood. She didn't speak to me. She hardly moved all the way back. I drove through the gates and up the sunken driveway to the *porte-cochère* of the big house. She jerked the car door open and was out of it before it had quite stopped. She didn't speak even then. I watched her back as she stood against the door after ringing the bell. The door opened and Norris looked out. She pushed past him quickly and was gone. The door banged shut and I was sitting there looking at it.

I turned back down the driveway and home.

24

The apartment house lobby was empty this time. No gunman waiting under the potted palm to give me orders. I took the automatic elevator up to my floor and walked along the hallway to the tune of a muted radio behind a door. I needed a drink and was in a hurry to get one. I didn't switch the light on inside the door. I made straight for the kitchenette and brought up short in three or four feet. Something was wrong. Something on the air, a scent. The shades were down at the windows and the street light leaking in at the sides made a dim light in the room. I stood still and listened. The scent on the air was a perfume, a heavy, cloying perfume.

There was no sound, no sound at all. Then my eyes adjusted themselves more to the darkness and I saw there was something across the floor in front of me that shouldn't have been there. I backed, reached the wall switch with my thumb and flicked the light on.

The bed was down. Something in it giggled. A blonde head was pressed into my pillow. Two bare arms curved up and the hands belonging to them were clasped on top of the blonde head. Carmen Sternwood lay on her back, in my bed, giggling at me. The tawny wave of her hair was spread out on the pillow as if by a careful and artificial hand. Her slaty eyes peered at me and had the effect, as usual, of peering from behind a barrel. She smiled. Her small sharp teeth glinted.

'Cute, aren't I?' she said.

I said harshly: 'Cute as a Filipino on Saturday night.'

I went over to a floor lamp and pulled the switch, went back to put off the ceiling light, and went across the room again to the chessboard on a card table under the lamp. There was a problem laid out on the board, a six-mover. I couldn't solve it, like a lot of my problems. I reached down and moved a knight, then pulled my hat and coat off and threw them somewhere. All this time the soft giggling went on from the bed, that sound that made me think of rats behind a wainscoting in an old house.

'I bet you can't even guess how I got in.'

I dug a cigarette out and looked at her with bleak eyes. 'I bet I can. You came through the keyhole, just like Peter Pan.'

'Who's he?'

'Oh, a fellow I used to know around the poolroom.'

She giggled. 'You're cute, aren't you?' she said.

I began to say: 'About that thumb – ' but she was ahead of me. I didn't have to remind her. She took her right hand from behind her head and started sucking the thumb and eyeing me with very round and naughty eyes.

'I'm all undressed,' she said, after I had smoked and stared at her for a minute.

'By God,' I said, 'it was right at the back of my mind.

I was groping for it. I almost had it, when you spoke. In another minute I'd have said "I bet you're all undressed." I always wear my rubbers in bed myself, in case I wake up with a bad conscience and have to sneak away from it.'

'You're cute.' She rolled her head a little, kittenishly. Then she took her left hand from under her head, and took hold of the covers, paused dramatically, and swept them aside. She was undressed all right. She lay there on the bed in the lamplight, as naked and glistening as a pearl. The Sternwood girls were giving me both barrels that night.

I pulled a shred of tobacco off the edge of my lower lip.

'That's nice,' I said. 'But I've already seen it all. Remember? I'm the guy that keeps finding you without any clothes on.'

She giggled some more and covered herself up again.

'Well, how *did* you get in?' I asked her.

'The manager let me in. I showed him your card. I'd stolen it from Vivian. I told him you told me to come here and wait for you. I was – I was mysterious.' She glowed with delight.

'Neat,' I said. 'Managers are like that. Now I know how you got in tell me how you're going to go out.'

She giggled. 'Not going – not for a long time . . . I like it here. You're cute.'

'Listen,' I pointed my cigarette at her. 'Don't make me dress you again. I'm tired. I appreciate all you're offering me. It's just more than I could possibly take. Doghouse Reilly never let a pal down that way. I'm your friend. I won't let you down – in spite of yourself. You and I have to keep on being friends, and this isn't the way to do it. Now will you dress like a nice little girl?'

She shook her head from side to side.

'Listen,' I ploughed on, 'you don't really care anything about me. You're just showing how naughty you can be. But you don't have to show me. I knew it already. I'm the guy that found –'

'Put the light out,' she giggled.

I threw my cigarette on the floor and stamped on it. I took a handkerchief out and wiped the palms of my hands. I tried it once more.

'It isn't on account of the neighbours,' I told her. 'They don't really care a lot. There's a lot of stray broads in any apartment house and one more won't make the building rock. It's a question of professional pride. You know – professional pride. I'm working for your father. He's a sick man, very frail, very helpless. He sort of trusts me not to pull any stunts. Won't you please get dressed, Carmen?'

'Your name isn't Doghouse Reilly,' she said. 'It's Philip Marlowe. You can't fool me.'

I looked down at the chessboard. The move with the knight was wrong. I put it back where I had moved it from. Knights had no meaning in this game. It wasn't a game for knights.

I looked at her again. She lay still now, her face pale against the pillow, her eyes large and dark and empty as rain barrels in a drought. One of her small five-fingered thumbless hands picked at the cover restlessly. There was a vague glimmer of doubt starting to get born in her somewhere. She didn't know about it yet. It's so hard for women – even nice women – to realize that their bodies are not irresistible.

I said: 'I'm going out in the kitchen and mix a drink. Want one?'

'Uh-huh.' Dark silent mystified eyes stared at me solemnly, the doubt growing larger in them, creeping into them noiselessly, like a cat in long grass stalking a young blackbird.

'If you're dressed when I get back, you'll get the drink. Okey?'

Her teeth parted and a faint hissing noise came out of her mouth. She didn't answer me. I went out to the kitchenette and got out some Scotch and fizzwater and mixed a couple of highballs. I didn't have anything really exciting to drink, like nitroglycerine or distilled tigers' breath. She hadn't moved when I got back with the glasses. The hissing had stopped. Her eyes were dead again. Her lips started to smile at me. Then she sat up suddenly and threw all the covers off her body and reached.

'Gimme.'

'When you're dressed. Not *until* you're dressed.'

I put the two glasses down on the card table and sat down myself and lit another cigarette. 'Go ahead. I won't watch you.'

I looked away. Then I was aware of the hissing noise very sudden and sharp. It startled me into looking at her again. She sat there naked, propped on her hands, her mouth open a little, her face like scraped bone. The hissing noise came tearing out of her mouth as if she had nothing to do with it. There was something behind her eyes, blank as they were, that I had never seen in a woman's eyes.

Then her lips moved very slowly and carefully, as if they were artificial lips and had to be manipulated with springs.

She called me a filthy name.

I didn't mind that. I didn't mind what she called me, what anybody called me. But this was the room I had to live in. It was all I had in the way of a home. In it was everything that was mine, that had any association for me, any past, anything that took the place of a family. Not much; a few books, pictures, radio, chessmen, old letters, stuff like that. Nothing. Such as they were they had all my memories.

I couldn't stand her in that room any longer. What she called me only reminded me of that.

I said carefully: 'I'll give you three minutes to get dressed and out of here. If you're not out by then, I'll throw you out – by force. Just the way you are, naked. And I'll throw your clothes after you into the hall. Now – get started.'

Her teeth chattered and the hissing noise was sharp and animal. She swung her feet to the floor and reached for her clothes on a chair beside the bed. She dressed. I watched her. She dressed with stiff awkward fingers – for a woman – but quickly at that. She was dressed in a little over two minutes. I timed it.

She stood there beside the bed, holding a green bag tight against a fur-trimmed coat. She wore a rakish green hat crooked on her head. She stood there for a moment and hissed at me, her face still like scraped bone, her eyes still empty and yet full of some jungle emotion. Then she walked quickly to the door and opened it and went out, without speaking, without looking back. I heard the elevator lurch into motion and move in the shaft.

I walked to the windows and pulled the shades up and opened the windows wide. The night air came drifting in with a kind of stale sweetness that still remembered automobile exhausts and the streets of the city. I reached for my drink and drank it slowly. The apartment house door closed itself down below me. Steps tinkled on the quiet pavement. A car started up not far away. It rushed off into the night with a rough clashing of gears. I went back to the bed and looked down at it. The imprint of her head was still in the pillow, of her small corrupt body still on the sheets.

I put my empty glass down and tore the bed to pieces savagely.

25

It was raining again the next morning, a slanting grey rain like a swung curtain of crystal beads. I got up feeling sluggish and tired and stood looking out of the windows, with a dark harsh taste of Sternwoods still in my mouth. I was as empty of life as a scarecrow's pockets. I went out to the kitchenette and drank two cups of black coffee. You can have a hangover from other things than alcohol. I had one from women. Women made me sick.

I shaved and showered and dressed and got my raincoat out and went downstairs and looked out of the front door. Across the street, a hundred feet up, a grey Plymouth sedan was parked. It was the same one that had tried to trail me around the day before, the same one that I had asked Eddie Mars about. There might be a cop in it, if a cop had that much time on his hands and wanted to waste it following me around. Or it might be a smoothie in the detective business trying to get a noseful of somebody else's case in order to chisel a way into it. Or it might be the Bishop of Bermuda disapproving of my night life.

I went out back and got my convertible from the garage and drove it around front past the grey Plymouth. There was a small man in it, alone. He started up after me. He worked better in the rain. He stayed close enough so that I couldn't make a short block and leave that before he entered it, and he stayed back far enough so that other cars were between us most of the time. I drove down to the boulevard and parked in the lot next to my building and came out of there with my raincoat collar up and my hat brim low and the raindrops tapping icily at my face in between. The Plymouth was across the way at a fireplug. I walked down to the intersection and crossed with the green light and walked back, close to the edge of the pavement and the parked cars. The Plymouth hadn't moved. Nobody got out of it. I reached it and jerked open the door on the kerb side.

A small bright-eyed man was pressed back into the corner behind the wheel. I stood and looked in at him, the rain thumping my back. His eyes blinked behind the swirling smoke of a cigarette. His hands tapped restlessly on the thin wheel.

I said: 'Can't you make your mind up?'

He swallowed and the cigarette bobbed between his lips. 'I don't think I know you,' he said, in a tight little voice.

'Marlowe's the name. The guy you've been trying to follow around for a couple of days.'

'I ain't following anybody, doc.'

'This jaloppy is. Maybe you can't control it. Have it your own way. I'm now going to eat breakfast in the coffee shop across the street, orange juice, bacon and eggs, toast, honey, three or four cups of coffee, and a toothpick.

I am then going up to my office, which is on the seventh floor of the building right opposite you. If you have anything that's worrying you beyond endurance, drop up and chew it over. I'll only be oiling my machine-gun.'

I left him blinking and walked away. Twenty minutes later I was airing the scrubwoman's Soirée d'Amour out of my office and opening up a thick rough envelope addressed in a fine old-fashioned pointed handwriting. The envelope contained a brief formal note and a large mauve cheque for five hundred dollars, payable to Philip Marlowe and signed, Guy de Brisay Sternwood, by Vincent Norris. That made it a nice morning. I was making out a bank slip when the buzzer told me somebody had entered my two by four reception-room. It was the little man from the Plymouth.

'Fine,' I said. 'Come in and shed your coat.'

He slid past me carefully as I held the door, as carefully as though he feared I might plant a kick in his minute buttocks. We sat down and faced each other across the desk. He was a very small man, not more than five feet three and would hardly weigh as much as a butcher's thumb. He had tight brilliant eyes that wanted to look hard, and looked as hard as oysters on the half-shell. He wore a double-breasted dark grey suit that was too wide in the shoulders and had too much lapel. Over this, open, an Irish tweed coat with some badly worn spots. A lot of foulard tie bulged out and was rain-spotted above his crossed lapels.

'Maybe you know me,' he said. 'I'm Harry Jones.'

I said I didn't know him. I pushed a flat tin of cigarettes

at him. His small neat fingers speared one like a trout taking the fly. He lit it with the desk lighter and waved his hand.

'I been around,' he said. 'Know the boys and such. Used to do a little liquor-running down from Hueneme Point. A tough racket, brother. Riding the scout car with a gun in your lap and a wad on your hip that would choke a coal chute. Plenty of times we paid off four sets of law before we hit Beverly Hills. A tough racket.'

'Terrible,' I said.

He leaned back and blew smoke at the ceiling from the small tight corner of his small tight mouth.

'Maybe you don't believe me,' he said.

'Maybe I don't,' I said. 'And maybe I do. And then again maybe I haven't bothered to make my mind up. Just what is the build-up supposed to do to me?'

'Nothing,' he said tartly.

'You've been following me around for a couple of days,' I said. 'Like a fellow trying to pick up a girl and lacking the last inch of nerve. Maybe you're selling insurance. Maybe you knew a fellow called Joe Brody. That's a lot of maybes, but I have a lot on hand in my business.'

His eyes bulged and his lower lip almost fell in his lap. 'Christ, how'd you know that?' he said.

'I'm psychic. Shake your business up and pour it. I haven't got all day.'

The brightness of his eyes almost disappeared between the suddenly narrowed lids. There was silence. The rain pounded down on the flat tarred roof over the Mansion

House lobby below my windows. His eyes opened a little, shined again, and his voice was full of thought.

'I was trying to get a line on you, sure,' he said. 'I've got something to sell – cheap, for a couple of C notes. How'd you tie me to Joe?'

I opened a letter and read it. It offered me a six months' correspondence course in fingerprinting at a special professional discount. I dropped it into the waste basket and looked at the little man again. 'Don't mind me. I was just guessing. You're not a cop. You don't belong to Eddie Mars's outfit. I asked him last night. I couldn't think of anybody else but Joe Brody's friends who would be that much interested in me.'

'Jesus,' he said and licked his lower lip. His face had turned white as paper when I mentioned Eddie Mars. His mouth drooped open and his cigarette hung to the corner of it by some magic, as if it had grown there. 'Aw, you're kidding me,' he said at last, with the sort of smile the operating-room sees.

'All right. I'm kidding you.' I opened another letter. This one wanted to send me a daily news-letter from Washington, all inside stuff, straight from the cookhouse. 'I suppose Agnes is loose,' I added.

'Yeah. She sent me. You interested?'

'Well – she's a blonde.'

'Nuts. You made a crack when you were up there that night – the night Joe got squibbed off. Something about Brody must have known something good about the Sternwoods or he wouldn't have taken the chance on that picture he sent them.'

'Uh-huh. So he had? What was it?'

'That's what the two hundred bucks pays for.'

I dropped some more fan mail into the basket and lit myself a fresh cigarette.

'We gotta get out of town,' he said. 'Agnes is a nice girl. You can't hold that stuff on her. It's not so easy for a dame to get by these days.'

'She's too big for you,' I said. 'She'll roll on you and smother you.'

'That's kind of a dirty crack, brother,' he said with something that was near enough to dignity to make me stare at him.

I said: 'You're right. I've been meeting the wrong kind of people lately. Let's cut out the gabble and get down to cases. What have you got for the money?'

'Would you pay it?'

'If it does what?'

'If it helps you find Rusty Regan.'

'I'm not looking for Rusty Regan.'

'Says you. Want to hear it or not?'

'Go ahead and chirp. I'll pay for anything I use. Two C notes buys a lot of information in my circle.'

'Eddie Mars had Regan bumped off,' he said calmly, and leaned back as if he had just been made a vice-president.

I waved a hand in the direction of the door. 'I wouldn't even argue with you,' I said. 'I wouldn't waste the oxygen. On your way, small size.'

He leaned across the desk, white lines at the corners of his mouth. He snubbed his cigarette out carefully, over and over again, without looking at it. From behind a communicating door came the sound of a typewriter clacking monotonously to the bell, to the shift, line after line.

'I'm not kidding,' he said.

'Beat it. Don't bother me. I have work to do.'

'No you don't,' he said sharply. 'I ain't that easy. I came here to speak my piece and I'm speaking it. I knew Rusty myself. Not well, well enough to say "How's a boy?" and he'd answer me or he wouldn't, according to how he felt. A nice guy though. I always liked him. He was sweet on a singer named Mona Grant. Then she changed her name to Mars. Rusty got sore and married a rich dame that hung around the joints like she couldn't sleep well at home. You know all about her, tall, dark, enough looks for a Derby winner, but the type would put a lot of pressure on a guy. High-strung. Rusty wouldn't get along with her. But Jesus, he'd get along with her old man's dough, wouldn't he? That's what you think. This Regan was a cockeyed sort of buzzard. He had long-range eyes. He was looking over into the next valley all the time. He wasn't scarcely around where he was. I don't think he gave a damn about dough. And coming from me, brother, that's a compliment.'

The little man wasn't so dumb after all. A three for a quarter grifter wouldn't even think such thoughts, much less know how to express them.

I said: 'So he ran away.'

'He started to run away, maybe. With this girl Mona. She wasn't living with Eddie Mars, didn't like his rackets. Especially the side lines, like blackmail, bent cars, hideouts for hot boys from the east, and so on. The talk was Regan told Eddie one night, right out in the open, that if he ever messed Mona up in any criminal rap, he'd be around to see him.'

'Most of this is on the record, Harry,' I said. 'You can't expect money for that.'

'I'm coming to what isn't. So Regan blew. I used to see him every afternoon in Vardi's drinking Irish whisky and staring at the wall. He don't talk much any more. He'd give me a bet now and then, which was what I was there for, to pick up bets for Puss Walgreen.'

'I thought he was in the insurance business.'

'That's what it says on the door. I guess he'd sell you insurance at that, if you tramped on him. Well, about the middle of September I don't see Regan any more. I don't notice it right away. You know how it is. A guy's there and you see him and then he ain't there and you don't see him until something makes you think of it. What makes me think about it is I hear a guy say laughing that Eddie Mars's woman lammed out with Rusty Regan and Mars is acting like he was best man, instead of being sore. So I tell Joe Brody and Joe was smart.'

'Like hell he was,' I said.

'Not copper smart, but still smart. He's out for the dough. He gets to figuring could he get a line somehow on the two lovebirds he could maybe collect twice – once from Eddie Mars and once from Regan's wife. Joe knew the family a little.'

'Five grand worth,' I said. 'He nicked them for that a while back.'

'Yeah?' Harry Jones looked mildly surprised. 'Agnes

ought to have told me that. There's a frail for you. Always holding out. Well, Joe and me watch the papers and we don't see anything, so we know old Sternwood has a blanket on it. Then one day I see Lash Canino in Vardi's. Know him?'

I shook my head.

'There's a boy that is tough like some guys think they are tough. He does a job for Eddie Mars when Mars needs him – trouble-shooting. He'd bump a guy off between drinks. When Mars don't need him he don't go near him. And he don't stay in LA. Well it might be something and it might not. Maybe they got a line on Regan and Mars has just been sitting back with a smile on his puss, waiting for the chance. Then again it might be something else entirely. Anyway I tell Joe and Joe gets on Canino's tail. He can tail. Me, I'm no good at it. I'm giving that one away. No charge. And Joe tails Canino out to the Sternwood place and Canino parks outside the estate and a car comes up beside him with a girl in it. They talk for a while and Joe thinks the girl passes something over, like maybe dough. The girl beats it. It's Regan's wife. Okey, she knows Canino and Canino knows Mars. So Joe figures Canino knows something about Regan and is trying to squeeze a little on the side for himself. Canino blows and Joe loses him. End of Act One.'

'What does this Canino look like?'

'Short, heavy set, brown hair, brown eyes, and always wears brown clothes and a brown hat. Even wears a brown suede raincoat. Drives a brown coupé. Everything brown for Mr Canino.'

'Let's have Act Two,' I said.

'Without some dough that's all.'

'I don't see two hundred bucks in it. Mrs Regan married an ex-bootlegger out of the joints. She'd know other people of his sort. She knows Eddie Mars well. If she thought anything had happened to Regan, Eddie would be the very man she'd go to, and Canino might be the man Eddie would pick to handle the assignment. Is that all you have?'

'Would you give the two hundred to know where Eddie's wife is?' the little man asked calmly.

He had all my attention now. I almost cracked the arms of my chair leaning on them.

'Even if she was alone?' Harry Jones added in a soft, rather sinister tone. 'Even if she never run away with Regan at all, and was being kept now about forty miles from LA in a hideout – so the law would keep on thinking she had dusted with him? Would you pay two hundred bucks for that, shamus?'

I licked my lips. They tasted dry and salty. 'I think I would,' I said. 'Where?'

'Agnes found her,' he said grimly. 'Just by a lucky break. Saw her out riding and managed to tail her home. Agnes will tell you where that is – when she's holding the money in her hand.'

I made a hard face at him. 'You could tell the coppers for nothing, Harry. They have some good wreckers, down at Central these days. If they killed you trying, they still have Agnes.'

'Let 'em try,' he said. 'I ain't so brittle.'

'Agnes must have something I didn't notice.'

'She's a grifter, shamus. I'm a grifter. We're all grifters. So we sell each other out for a nickel. Okey. See can you make me.' He reached for another of my cigarettes, placed it neatly between his lips and lit it with a match the way I do myself, missing twice on his thumbnail and then using his foot. He puffed evenly and stared at me level-eyed, a funny little hard guy I could have thrown from home plate to second base. A small man in a big man's world. There was something I liked about him.

'I haven't pulled anything in here,' he said steadily. 'I came in talking two C's. That's still the price. I come because I thought I'd get a take it or leave it, one right gee to another. Now you're waving cops at me. You oughta be ashamed of yourself.'

I said: 'You'll get the two hundred – for that information. I have to get the money myself first.'

He stood up and nodded and pulled his worn little Irish tweed coat tight around his chest. 'That's okey. After dark is better anyway. It's a leery job – buckin' guys like Eddie Mars. But a guy has to eat. The book's been pretty dull lately. I think the big boys have told Puss Walgreen to move on. Suppose you come over there to the office, Fulwider Building, Western and Santa Monica, four-twenty-eight at the back. You bring the money, I'll take you to Agnes.'

'Can't you tell me yourself? I've seen Agnes.'

'I promised her,' he said simply. He buttoned his overcoat, cocked his hat jauntily, nodded again and strolled to the door. He went out. His steps died along the hall.

I went down to the bank and deposited my five-hundred-dollar cheque and drew out two hundred in currency. I went upstairs again and sat in my chair thinking about Harry Jones and his story. It seemed a little too pat. It had the austere simplicity of fiction rather than the tangled woof of fact. Captain Gregory ought to have been able to find Mona Mars, if she was that close to his beat. Supposing, that is, he had tried.

I thought about it most of the day. Nobody came into the office. Nobody called me on the phone. It kept on raining.

26

At seven the rain had stopped for a breathing spell, but the gutters were still flooded. On Santa Monica the water was level with the pavement and a thin film of it washed over the top of the kerbing. A traffic cop in shining black rubber from boots to cap sloshed through the flood on his way from the shelter of a sodden awning. My rubber heels slithered on the pavement as I turned into the narrow lobby of the Fulwider Building. A single drop light burned far back, beyond an open, once-gilt elevator. There was a tarnished and well-missed spittoon on a gnawed rubber mat. A case of false teeth hung on the mustard-coloured wall like a fuse box in a screen porch. I shook the rain off my hat and looked at the building directory beside the case of teeth. Numbers with names and numbers without names. Plenty of vacancies or plenty of tenants who wished to remain anonymous. Painless dentists, shyster detective agencies, small sick businesses that had crawled there to die, mail order schools that would teach you how to become a railway clerk or a radio technician or a screen writer – if the postal inspectors didn't catch up with them first. A nasty building. A building in which the smell of stale cigar butts would be the cleanest odour.

An old man dozed in the elevator, on a ramshackle stool, with a burst-out cushion under him. His mouth was open, his veined temples glistened in the weak light. He wore a blue uniform coat that fitted him the way a stall fits a horse. Under that grey trousers with frayed cuffs, white cotton socks and black kid shoes, one of which was slit across a bunion. On the stool he slept miserably, waiting for a customer. I went past him softly, the clandestine air of the building prompting me, found the fire door and pulled it open. The fire stairs hadn't been swept in a month. Bums had slept on them, eaten on them, left crusts and fragments of greasy newspaper, matches, a gutted imitation-leather pocket-book. In a shadowy angle against the scribbled wall a pouched ring of pale rubber had fallen and had not been disturbed. A very nice building.

I came out at the fourth floor sniffing for air. The hallway had the same dirty spittoon and frayed mat, the same mustard walls, the same memories of low tide. I went down the line and turned a corner. The name: 'L. D. Walgreen – Insurance,' showed on a dark pebbled glass door, on a second dark door, on a third behind which there was a light. One of the dark doors said: 'Entrance.'

A glass transom was open above the lighted door. Through it the sharp birdlike voice of Harry Jones spoke, saying:

'Canino? . . . Yeah, I've seen you around somewhere. Sure.'

I froze. The other voice spoke. It had a heavy purr, like

a small dynamo behind a brick wall. It said: 'I thought you would.' There was a vaguely sinister note in that voice.

A chair scraped on linoleum, steps sounded, the transom above me squeaked shut. A shadow melted from behind the pebbled glass.

I went back to the first of the three doors marked with the name Walgreen. I tried it cautiously. It was locked. It moved in a loose frame, an old door fitted many years past, made of half-seasoned wood and shrunken now. I reached my wallet out and slipped the thick hard window of celluloid from over my driver's licence. A burglar's tool the law had forgotten to proscribe. I put my gloves on, leaned softly and lovingly against the door and pushed the knob hard away from the frame. I pushed the celluloid plate into the wide crack and felt for the slope of the spring lock. There was a dry click, like a small icicle breaking. I hung there motionless, like a lazy fish in the water. Nothing happened inside. I turned the knob and pushed the door back into darkness. I shut it behind me as carefully as I had opened it.

The lighted oblong of an uncurtained window faced me, cut by the angle of a desk. On the desk a hooded typewriter took form, then the metal knob of a communicating door. This was unlocked. I passed into the second of the three offices. Rain rattled suddenly against the closed window. Under its noise I crossed the room. A tight fan of light spread from an inch opening of the door into the lighted office. Everything very convenient. I walked like a cat on a mantel and reached the hinged side of the door, put an eye to the crack and saw nothing but light against the angle of the wood.

The purring voice was now saying quite pleasantly: 'Sure, a guy could sit on his fanny and crab what another guy done if he knows what it's all about. So you go to see this peeper. Well, that was your mistake. Eddie don't like it. The peeper told Eddie some guy in a grey Plymouth was tailing him. Eddie naturally wants to know who and why, see.'

Harry Jones laughed lightly. 'What makes it his business?'

'That don't get you no place.'

'You know why I went to the peeper. I already told you. Account of Joe Brody's girl. She has to blow and she's shatting on her uppers. She figures the peeper can get her some dough. I don't have any.'

The purring voice said gently: 'Dough for what? Peepers don't give that stuff out to punks.'

'He could raise it. He knows rich people.' Harry Jones laughed, a brave little laugh.

'Don't fuss with me, little man.' The purring voice had an edge, like sand in the bearings.

'Okey, okey. You know the dope on Brody's bump-off. That screwy kid done it all right, but the night it happened this Marlowe was right there in the room.'

'That's known, little man. He told it to the law.'

'Yeah – here's what isn't. Brody was trying to peddle a nudist photo of the young Sternwood girl. Marlowe got wise to him. While they were arguing about it the young Sternwood girl dropped around herself – with a gat. She took a shot at Brody. She lets one fly and breaks a window. Only the peeper didn't tell the coppers about that. And Agnes didn't neither. She figures it's railway fare for her not to.'

'This ain't got anything to do with Eddie?'

'Show me how.'

'Where's this Agnes at?'

'Nothing doing.'

'You'll tell me, little man. Here, or in the back room where the boys pitch dimes against the wall.'

'She's my girl now, Canino. I don't put my girl in the middle for anybody.'

A silence followed. I listened to the rain lashing the windows. The smell of cigarette smoke came through the crack of the door. I wanted to cough. I bit hard on a handkerchief.

The purring voice said, still gentle: 'From what I hear this blonde broad was just a shill for Geiger. I'll talk it over with Eddie. How much you tap the peeper for?'

'Two centuries.'

'Get it?'

Harry Jones laughed again. 'I'm seeing him to-morrow. I have hopes.'

'Where's Agnes?'

'Listen –'

'Where's Agnes?'

Silence.

'Look at it, little man.'

I didn't move. I wasn't wearing a gun. I didn't have to see through the crack of the door to know that a gun was what the purring voice was inviting Harry Jones to look at. But I didn't think Mr Canino would do anything with his gun beyond showing it. I waited.

'I'm looking at it,' Harry Jones said, his voice squeezed tight as if it could hardly get past his teeth. 'And I don't see anything I didn't see before. Go ahead and blast and see what it gets you.'

'A Chicago overcoat is what it would get *you*, little man.'

Silence.

'Where's Agnes?'

Harry Jones sighed. 'Okey,' he said wearily. 'She's in an apartment house at 28 Court Street, up on Bunker Hill. Apartment 301. I guess I'm yellow all right. Why should I front for that twist?'

'No reason. You got good sense. You and me'll go out and talk to her. All I want is to find out is she dummying up on you, kid. If it's the way you say it is, everything is jakeloo. You can put the bite on the peeper and be on your way. No hard feelings?'

'No,' Harry Jones said. 'No hard feelings, Canino.'

'Fine. Let's dip the bill. Got a glass?' The purring voice was now as false as an usherette's eyelashes and as slippery as a watermelon seed. A drawer was pulled open. Something jarred on wood. A chair squeaked. A scuffing sound on the floor. 'This is bond stuff,' the purring voice said.

There was a gurgling sound. 'Moths in your ermine, as the ladies say.'

Harry Jones said softly: 'Success.'

I heard a short sharp cough. Then a violent retching.

There was a small thud on the floor, as if a thick glass had fallen. My fingers curled against my raincoat.

The purring voice said gently: 'You ain't sick from just one drink, are you, pal?'

Harry Jones didn't answer. There was laboured breathing for a short moment. Then thick silence folded down. Then a chair scraped.

'So long, little man,' said Mr Canino.

Steps, a click, the wedge of light died at my feet, a door opened and closed quietly. The steps faded, leisurely and assured.

I stirred around the edge of the door and pulled it wide and looked into blackness relieved by the dim shine of a window. The corner of a desk glittered faintly. A hunched shape took form in a chair behind it. In the close air there was a heavy clogged smell, almost a perfume. I went across to the corridor and listened. I heard the distant clang of the elevator.

I found the light switch and light glowed in a dusty glass bowl hanging from the ceiling by three brass chains. Harry Jones looked at me across the desk, his eyes wide open, his face frozen in a tight spasm, the skin bluish. His small dark head was tilted to one side. He sat upright against the back of the chair.

A tramcar bell clanged at an almost infinite distance and the sound came buffeted by innumerable walls. A brown half-pint of whisky stood on the desk with the cap off. Harry Jones's glass glinted against a castor of the desk. The second glass was gone.

I breathed shallowly, from the top of my lungs, and

bent above the bottle. Behind the charred smell of the bourbon another odour lurked, faintly, the odour of bitter almonds. Harry Jones dying had vomited on his coat. That made it cyanide.

I walked around him carefully and lifted a phone book from a hook on the wooden frame of the window. I let it fall again, reached the telephone as far as it would go from the little dead man. I dialled information. The voice answered.

'Can you give me the phone number of Apartment 301, 28 Court Street?'

'One moment, please.' The voice came to me borne on the smell of bitter almonds. A silence. 'The number is Wentworth 2528. It is listed under Glendower Apartments.'

I thanked the voice and dialled the number. The bell rang three times, then the line opened. A radio blared along the wire and was muted. A burly male voice said: 'Hello.'

'Is Agnes there?'

'No Agnes here, buddy. What number you want?'

'Wentworth two-five-two-eight.'

'Right number, wrong gal. Ain't that a shame?' The voice cackled.

I hung up and reached for the phone book again and looked up the Wentworth Apartments. I dialled the manager's number. I had a blurred vision of Mr Canino driving fast through rain to another appointment with death.

'Glendower Apartments. Mr Schiff speaking.'

'This is Wallis, Police Identification Bureau. Is there a girl named Agnes Lozelle registered in your place?'

'Who did you say you were?'

I told him again.

'If you'll give me your number I'll –'

'Cut the comedy,' I said sharply, 'I'm in a hurry. Is there or isn't there?'

'No. There isn't.' The voice was as stiff as a bread-stick.

'Is there a tall blonde with green eyes registered in the flop?'

'Say, this isn't any flop –'

'Oh, can it, *can it!*' I rapped at him in a police voice. 'You want me to send the vice squad over there and shake the joint down? I know all about Bunker Hill apartment houses, mister. Especially the ones that have phone numbers listed for each apartment.'

'Hey, take it easy, officer. I'll co-operate. There's a couple of blondes here, sure. Where isn't there? I hadn't noticed their eyes much. Would yours be alone?'

'Alone, or with a little chap about five feet three, a hundred and ten, sharp black eyes, wears double-breasted dark grey suit and Irish tweed overcoat, grey hat. My information is Apartment 301, but all I get there is the big razzoo.'

'Oh, she ain't there. There's a couple of car salesmen living in three-o-one.'

'Thanks, I'll drop around.'

'Make it quiet, won't you? Come to my place, direct?'

'Much obliged, Mr Schiff.' I hung up.

I wiped sweat off my face. I walked to the far corner of the office and stood with my face to the wall, patted it with a hand. I turned around slowly and looked across at little Harry Jones grimacing in his chair.

'Well, you fooled him, Harry,' I said out loud, in a voice that sounded queer to me. 'You lied to him and you drank your cyanide like a little gentleman. You died like a poisoned rat, Harry, but you're no rat to me.'

I had to search him. It was a nasty job. His pockets yielded nothing about Agnes, nothing that I wanted at all. I didn't think they would, but I had to be sure. Mr Canino might be back. Mr Canino would be the kind of self-confident gentleman who would not mind returning to the scene of his crime.

I put the light out and started to open the door. The phone bell rang jarringly down on the base-board. I listened to it, my jaw muscles drawn into a knot, aching. Then I shut the door and put the light on again and went across to it.

'Yeah?'

A woman's voice. Her voice. 'Is Harry around?'

'Not for a minute, Agnes.'

She waited a while on that. Then she said slowly: 'Who's talking?'

'Marlowe, the guy that's trouble to you.'

'Where is he?' sharply.

'I came over to give him two hundred bucks in return for certain information. The offer holds. I have the money. Where are you?'

'Didn't he tell you?'

'No.'

'Perhaps you'd better ask him. Where is he?'

'I can't ask him. Do you know a man named Canino?'

Her gasp came as clearly as though she had been beside me.

'Do you want the two C's or not?' I asked.

'I – I want it pretty bad, mister.'

'All right then. Tell me where to bring it.'

'I – I –' Her voice trailed off and came back with a panic rush. 'Where's Harry?'

'Got scared and blew. Meet me somewhere – anywhere at all – I have the money.'

'I don't believe you – about Harry. It's a trap.'

'Oh stuff. I could have had Harry hauled in long ago. There isn't anything to make a trap for. Canino got a line on Harry somehow and he blew. I want quiet, you want quiet, Harry wants quiet.' Harry already had it. Nobody could take it away from him. 'You don't think I'd stooge for Eddie Mars, do you, angel?'

'No-o, I guess not. Not that. I'll meet you in half an hour. Beside Bullocks Wilshire, the east entrance to the parking lot.'

'Right,' I said.

I dropped the phone in its cradle. The wave of almond odour flooded me again, and the sour smell of vomit. The little dead man sat silent in his chair, beyond fear, beyond change.

I left the office. Nothing moved in the dingy corridor. No pebbled glass door had light behind it. I went down the fire stairs to the second floor and from there looked down at the lighted roof of the elevator cage. I pressed the button. Slowly the car lurched into motion. I ran down the stairs again. The car was above me when I walked out of the building.

It was raining hard again. I walked into it with the heavy drops slapping my face. When one of them touched my tongue I knew that my mouth was open and the ache at the side of my jaws told me it was open wide and strained back, mimicking the rictus of death carved upon the face of Harry Jones.

27

'Give me the money.'

The motor of the grey Plymouth throbbed under her voice and the rain pounded above it. The violet light at the top of Bullocks green-tinged tower was far above us, serene and withdrawn from the dark, dripping city. Her black-gloved hand reached out and I put the bills in it. She bent over to count them under the dim light of the dash. A bag clicked open, clicked shut. She let a spent breath die on her lips. She leaned towards me.

'I'm leaving, copper. I'm on my way. This is a get-away stake and God how I need it. What happened to Harry?'

'I told you he ran away. Canino got wise to him somehow. Forget Harry. I've paid and I want my information.'

'You'll get it. Joe and I were out riding Foothill Boulevard Sunday before last. It was late and the lights coming up and the usual mess of cars. We passed a brown coupé and I saw the girl who was driving it. There was a man beside her, a dark short man. The girl was a blonde. I'd seen her before. She was Eddie Mars's wife. The guy was Canino. You wouldn't forget either of them, if you ever saw them. Joe tailed the coupé from in front. He was good at that. Canino, the watch-dog, was taking her out for air. A mile or so east of Realito a road turns towards the foothills. That's orange country to the south but to the north it's as bare as hell's back yard and smack up against the hills there's a cyanide plant where they make the stuff for fumigation. Just off the highway there's a small garage and paint-shop run by a gee named Art Huck. Hot car drop, likely. There's a frame house beyond this, and beyond the house nothing but the foothills and the bare stone outcrop and the cyanide plant a couple of miles on. That's the place where she's holed up. They turned off on this road and Joe swung around and went back and we saw the car turn off the road where the frame house was. We sat there half an hour looking through the cars going by. Nobody came back out. When it was quite dark Joe sneaked up there and took a look. He said there were lights in the house and a radio was going and just the one car out in front, the coupé. So we beat it.'

She stopped talking and I listened to the swish of tyres on Wilshire. I said: 'They might have shifted quarters since then but that's what you have to sell – that's what you have to sell. Sure you knew her?'

'If you ever see her, you won't make a mistake the second time. Good-bye, copper, and wish me luck. I got a raw deal.'

'Like hell you did,' I said, and walked away across the street to my own car.

The grey Plymouth moved forward, gathered speed, and darted around the corner on to Sunset Place. The sound of its motor died, and with it blonde Agnes wiped herself off the slate for good, so far as I was concerned. Three men dead, Geiger, Brody, and Harry Jones, and the woman went riding off in the rain with my two hundred in her bag and not a mark on her. I kicked my starter and drove on down-town to eat. I ate a good dinner. Forty miles in the rain is a hike, and I hoped to make it a round trip.

I drove north across the river, on into Pasadena, through Pasadena and almost at once I was in orange groves. The tumbling rain was solid white spray in the headlights. The windshield wiper could hardly keep the glass clear enough to see through. But not even the drenched darkness could hide the flawless lines of the orange trees wheeling away like endless spokes into the night.

Cars passed with a tearing hiss and a wave of dirty spray. The highway jerked through a little town that was all packing houses and sheds, and railway sidings nuzzling them. The groves thinned out and dropped away to the south and the road climbed and it was cold and to the north the black foothills crouched closer and sent a bitter wind whipping down their flanks. Then faintly out of the dark two yellow vapour lights glowed high up in the air and a neon sign between them said: 'Welcome to Realito.'

Frame houses were spaced far back from a wide main street, then a sudden knot of stores, the lights of a drugstore behind fogged glass, the fly-cluster of cars in front of a movie theatre, a dark bank on a corner with a clock sticking out over the pavement and a group of people standing in the rain looking at its windows, as if they were some kind of a show. I went on. Empty fields closed in again.

Fate stage-managed the whole thing. Beyond Realito, just about a mile beyond, the highway took a curve and the rain fooled me and I went too close to the shoulder. My right front tyre let go with an angry hiss. Before I could stop the right rear went with it. I jammed the car to a stop, half on the pavement, half on the shoulder, got out and flashed a spotlight around. I had two flats and one spare. The flat butt of a heavy galvanized tack stared at me from the front tyre. The edge of the pavement was littered with them. They had been swept off, but not far enough off.

I snapped the flash off and stood there breathing rain and looking up a side road at a yellow light. It seemed to come from a skylight. The skylight could belong to a garage, the garage could be run by a man named Art Huck, and there could be a frame house next door to it. I tucked my chin down in my collar and started towards it, then went back to unstrap the licence holder from the steering post and put it in my pocket. I leaned lower under the wheel. Behind a weighted flap, directly under my right leg as I sat in the car, there was a hidden compartment. There were two guns in it. One belonged to Eddie Mars's boy Lanny and one belonged to me. I took Lanny's. It would have had more practice than mine. I stuck it nose down in an inside pocket and started up the side road.

The garage was a hundred yards from the highway. It showed the highway a blank side wall. I played the flash on it quickly. 'Art Huck – Motor Repairs and Painting.' I chuckled, then Harry Jones's face rose up in front of me, and I stopped chuckling. The garage doors were shut, but there was an edge of light under them and a thread of light where the halves met. I went on past. The frame house was there, light in two front windows, shades down. It was set well back from the road, behind a thin clump of trees. A car stood on the gravel drive in front. It was dark, indistinct, but it would be a brown coupé and it would belong to Mr Canino. It squatted there peacefully in front of the narrow wooden porch.

He would let her take it out for a spin once in a while, and sit beside her, probably with a gun handy. The girl Rusty Regan ought to have married, that Eddie Mars couldn't keep, the girl that hadn't run away with Regan. Nice Mr Canino.

I trudged back to the garage and banged on the wooden door with the butt of my flash. There was a hung instant of silence, as heavy as thunder. The light inside went out. I stood there grinning and licking the rain off my lip. I clicked the spot on the middle of the doors. I grinned at the circle of white. I was where I wanted to be.

A voice spoke through the door, a surly voice: 'What you want?'

'Open up. I've got two flats back on the highway and only one spare. I need help.'

'Sorry, mister. We're closed up. Realito's a mile west. Better try there.'

I didn't like that. I kicked the door hard. I kept on kicking it. Another voice made itself heard, a purring voice, like a small dynamo behind a wall. I liked this voice. It said: 'A wise guy, huh? Open up, Art.'

A bolt squealed and half of the door bent inward. My flash burned briefly on a gaunt face. Then something that glittered swept down and knocked the flash out of my hand. A gun had peaked at me. I dropped low where the flash burned on the wet ground and picked it up.

The surly voice said: 'Kill that spot, bo. Folks get hurt that way.'

I snapped the flash off and straightened. Light went on inside the garage, outlined a tall man in overalls. He backed away from the open door and kept a gun levelled at me.

'Step inside and shut the door, stranger. We'll see what we can do.'

I stepped inside, and shut the door behind my back. I looked at the gaunt man, but not at the other man who was shadowy over by a workbench, silent. The breath of the garage was sweet and sinister with the smell of hot pyroxylin paint.

'Ain't you got no sense?' the gaunt man chided me. 'A bank job was pulled at Realito this noon.'

'Pardon,' I said, remembering the people staring at the bank in the rain. 'I didn't pull it. I'm a stranger here.'

'Well, there was,' he said morosely. 'Some say it was a couple of punk kids and they got 'em cornered back here in the hills.'

'It's a nice night for hiding,' I said. 'I suppose they threw tacks out. I got some of them. I thought you just needed the business.'

hips exactly where they had been before. I could have taken him then. We were alone. He didn't know who I was. He looked at me lightly and threw his cigarette on the cement floor and stamped on it without looking down.

'I bet you could use a drink,' he said. 'Wet the inside and even up. He reached a bottle from the workbench behind him and set it on the edge and set two glasses beside it. He poured a stiff jolt into each and held one out.

Walking like a dummy I went over and took it. The memory of the rain was still cold on my face. The smell of hot paint drugged the close air of the garage.

'That Art,' the brown man said. 'He's like all mechanics. Always got his face in a job he ought to have done last week. Business trip?'

I sniffed my drink delicately. It had the right smell. I watched him drink some of his before I swallowed mine. I rolled it around on my tongue. There was no cyanide in it. I emptied the little glass and put it down beside him and moved away.

'Partly,' I said. I walked over to the half-painted sedan with the big metal paint gun lying along its fender. The rain hit the flat roof hard. Art was out in it, cursing.

The brown man looked at the big car. 'Just a panel job, to start with,' he said casually, his purring voice still softer from the drink. 'But the guy had dough and his driver needed a few bucks. You know the racket.'

I said: 'There's only one that's older.' My lips felt dry. I didn't want to talk. I lit a cigarette. I wanted my tyres fixed. The minutes passed on tiptoe. The brown man and I were two strangers chance-met, looking at each other across a little dead man named Harry Jones. Only the brown man didn't know that yet.

Feet crunched outside and the door was pushed open. The light hit pencils of rain and made silver wires of them. Art trundled two muddy flats in sullenly, kicked the door shut, let one of the flats fall over on its side. He looked at me savagely.

'You sure pick spots for a jack to stand on,' he snarled.

The brown man laughed and took a rolled cylinder of nickels out of his pocket and tossed it up and down on the palm of his hand.

'Don't crab so much,' he said dryly. 'Fix those flats.'

'I'm fixin' them, ain't I?'

'Well, don't make a song about it.'

'Yah!' Art peeled his rubber coat and sou'wester off and threw them away from him. He heaved one tyre up on a spreader and tore the rim loose viciously. He had the tube out and cold-patched in nothing flat. Still scowling, he strode over to the wall beside me and grabbed an air hose, put enough air into the tube to give it body and let the nozzle of the air hose smack against the whitewashed wall.

I stood watching the roll of wrapped coins dance in Canino's hand. The moment of crouched intensity had left me. I turned my head and watched the gaunt mechanic beside me toss the air-stiffened tube up and catch it with his hands wide, one on each side of the tube. He looked it over sourly, glanced at a big galvanized tub of dirty water in the corner and grunted.

The teamwork must have been very nice. I saw no

signal, no glance of meaning, no gesture that might have a special import. The gaunt man had the stiffened tube high in the air, staring at it. He half turned his body, took one long quick step, and slammed it down over my head and shoulders, a perfect ringer.

He jumped behind me and leaned hard on the rubber. His weight dragged on my chest, pinned my upper arms tight to my sides. I could move my hands, but I couldn't reach the gun in my pocket.

The brown man came almost dancing towards me across the floor. His hand tightened over the roll of nickels. He came up to me without sound, without expression. I bent forward and tried to heave Art off his feet.

The fist with the weighted tube inside it went through my spread hands like a stone through a cloud of dust. I had the stunned moment of shock when the lights danced and the visible world went out of focus but was still there. He hit me again. There was no sensation in my head. The bright glare got brighter. There was nothing but hard aching white light. Then there was darkness in which something red wriggled like a germ under a microscope. Then there was nothing bright or wriggling, just darkness and emptiness and a rushing wind and a falling as of great trees.

28

It seemed there was a woman and she was sitting near a lamp, which was where she belonged, in a good light. Another light shone hard on my face, so I closed my eyes again and tried to look at her through the lashes. She was so platinumed that her hair shone like a silver fruit bowl. She wore a green knitted dress with a broad white collar turned over it. There was a sharp-angled glossy bag at her feet. She was smoking and a glass of amber fluid was tall and pale at her elbow.

I moved my head a little, carefully. It hurt, but not more than I expected. I was trussed like a turkey ready for the oven. Handcuffs held my wrists behind me and a rope went from them to my ankles and then over the end of the brown davenport on which I was sprawled. The rope dropped out of sight over the davenport. I moved enough to make sure it was tied down.

I stopped these furtive movements and opened my eyes again and said: 'Hello.'

The woman withdrew her gaze from some distant mountain peak. Her small firm chin turned slowly. Her eyes were the blue of mountain lakes. Overhead the rain still pounded, with a remote sound, as if it was somebody else's rain.

'How do you feel?' It was a smooth silvery voice that matched her hair. It had a tiny tinkle in it, like bells in a doll's house. I thought that was silly as soon as I thought of it.

'Great,' I said. 'Somebody built a filling station on my jaw.'

'What did you expect, Mr Marlowe – orchids?'

'Just a plain pine box,' I said. 'Don't bother with bronze or silver handles. And don't scatter my ashes over the blue Pacific. I like the worms better. Did you know that worms are of both sexes and that any worm can love any other worm?'

'You're a little light-headed,' she said, with a grave stare.

'Would you mind moving this light?'

She got up and went behind the davenport. The light went off. The dimness was a benison.

'I don't think you're so dangerous,' she said. She was tall rather than short, but no bean-pole. She was slim, but not a dried crust. She went back to her chair.

'So you know my name.'

'You slept well. They had plenty of time to go through your pockets. They did everything but embalm you. So you're a detective.'

'Is that all they have on me?'

She was silent. Smoke floated dimly from the cigarette. She moved it in the air. Her hand was small and had shape, not the usual bony garden tool you see on women nowadays.

'What time is it?' I asked.

She looked sideways at her wrist, beyond the spiral of smoke, at the edge of the grave lustre of the lamplight. 'Ten-seventeen. You have a date?'

'I wouldn't be surprised. Is this the house next to Art Huck's garage?'

'Yes.'

'What are the boys doing – digging a grave?'

'They had to go somewhere.'

'You mean they left you here alone?'

Her head turned slowly again. She smiled. 'You don't look dangerous.'

'I thought they were keeping you a prisoner.'

It didn't seem to startle her. It even slightly amused her. 'What made you think that?'

'I know who you are.'

Her very blue eyes flashed so sharply that I could almost see the sweep of their glance, like the sweep of a sword. Her mouth tightened. But her voice didn't change.

'Then I'm afraid you're in a bad spot. And I hate killing.'

'And you Eddie Mars's wife? Shame on you.'

She didn't like that. She glared at me. I grinned. 'Unless you can unlock these bracelets, which I'd advise you not to do, you might spare me a little of that drink you're neglecting.'

She brought the glass over. Bubbles rose in it like false hopes. She bent over me. Her breath was as delicate as the eyes of a fawn. I gulped from the glass. She took it away from my mouth and watched some of the liquid run down my neck.

She bent over me again. Blood began to move around in me, like a prospective tenant looking over a house.

'Your face looks like a collision mat,' she said.

'Make the most of it. It won't last long even this good.'

She swung her head sharply and listened. For an instant her face was pale. The sounds were only the rain drifting against the walls. She went back across the room and stood with her side to me, bent forward a little, looking down at the floor.

'Why did you come here and stick your neck out?' she asked quietly. 'Eddie wasn't doing you any harm. You know perfectly well that if I hadn't hid out here, the police would have been certain Eddie murdered Rusty Regan.'

'He did,' I said.

She didn't move, didn't change position an inch. Her breath made a harsh quick sound. I looked around the room. Two doors, both in the same wall, one half open. A carpet of red and tan squares, blue curtains at the windows, a wallpaper with bright green pine trees on it. The furniture looked as if it had come from one of those places that advertise on bus benches. Gay, but full of resistance.

She said softly: 'Eddie didn't do anything to him. I haven't seen Rusty in months. Eddie's not that sort of man.'

'You left his bed and board. You were living alone.

People at the place where you lived identified Regan's photo.'

'That's a lie,' she said coldly.

I tried to remember whether Captain Gregory had said that or not. My head was too fuzzy. I couldn't be sure.

'And it's none of your business,' she added.

'The whole thing is my business. I'm hired to find out.'

'Eddie's not that sort of man.'

'Oh, you like racketeers.'

'As long as people will gamble there will be places for them to gamble.'

'That's just protective thinking. Once outside the law you're all the way outside. You think he's just a gambler. I think he's a pornographer, a blackmailer, a hot car broker, a killer by remote control, and a suborner of crooked cops. He's whatever looks good to him, whatever has the cabbage pinned to it. Don't try to sell me on any high-souled racketeers. They don't come in that pattern.'

'He's not a killer.' She frowned.

'Not personally. He has Canino. Canino killed a man tonight, a harmless little guy who was trying to help somebody out. I almost saw him killed.'

She laughed wearily.

'All right,' I growled. 'Don't believe it. If Eddie is such a nice guy, I'd like to get to talk to him without Canino around. You know what Canino will do – beat my teeth out and then kick me in the stomach for mumbling.'

She put her head back and stood there thoughtful and withdrawn, thinking something out.

'I thought platinum hair was out of style,' I went on, just to keep sound alive in the room, just to keep from listening.

'It's a wig, silly. While mine grows out.' She reached up and yanked if off. Her own hair was clipped short all over, like a boy's. She put the wig back on.

'Who did that to you?'

She looked surprised. 'I had it done. Why?'

'Yes. Why?'

'Why, to show Eddie I was willing to do what he wanted me to do – hide out. That he didn't need to have me guarded. I wouldn't let him down. I love him.'

'Good grief,' I groaned. 'And you have me right here in the room with you.'

She turned a hand over and stared at it. Then abruptly she walked out of the room. She came back with a kitchen knife. She bent and sawed at my rope.

'Canino has the key to the handcuffs,' she said. 'I can't do anything about those.'

She stepped back, breathing rapidly. She had cut the rope at every knot.

'You're a kick,' she said. 'Kidding with every breath – the spot you're in.'

'I thought Eddie wasn't a killer.'

She turned away quickly and went back to her chair by the lamp and sat down and put her face in her hands. I swung my feet to the floor and stood up. I tottered around, stiff-legged. The nerve on the left side of my face was jumping in all its branches. I took a step. I could still walk. I could run, if I had to.

'I guess you mean me to go,' I said.

She nodded without lifting her head.

'You'd better go with me – if you want to keep on living.'

'Don't waste time. He'll be back any minute.'

'Light a cigarette for me.'

I stood beside her, touching her knees. She came to her feet with a sudden lurch. Our eyes were only inches apart.

'Hello, Silver-Wig,' I said softly.

She stepped back, around the chair, and swept a package of cigarettes up off the table. She jabbed one loose and pushed it roughly into my mouth. Her hand was shaking. She snapped a small green leather lighter and held it to the cigarette. I drew in the smoke, staring into her lake-blue eyes. While she was still close to me I said:

'A little bird named Harry Jones led me to you. A little bird that used to hop in and out of cocktail bars picking up horse bets for crumbs. Picking up information too. This little bird picked up an idea about Canino. One way and another he and his friends found out where you were. He came to me to sell the information because he knew – how he knew is a long story – that I was working for General Sternwood. I got his information, but Canino got the little bird. He's a dead little bird now, with his feathers ruffled and his neck limp and a pearl of blood on his beak. Canino killed him. But Eddie Mars wouldn't do that, would he, Silver-Wig? He never killed anybody. He just hires it done.'

'Get out,' she said harshly. 'Get out of here quick.'

Her hand clutched in midair on the green lighter. The fingers strained. The knuckles were as white as snow.

'But Canino doesn't know I know that,' I said. 'About the little bird. All he knows is I'm nosing around.'

Then she laughed. It was almost a racking laugh. It shook her as the wind shakes a tree. I thought there was puzzlement in it, not exactly surprise, but as if a new idea had been added to something already known and it didn't fit. Then I thought that was too much to get out of a laugh.

'It's very funny,' she said breathlessly. 'Very funny, because, you see – I still love him. Women –.' She began to laugh again.

I listened hard, my head throbbing. 'Let's go,' I said. 'Fast.'

She took two steps back and her face set hard. 'Get out, you! Get out! You can walk to Realito. You can make it – and you can keep your mouth shut – for an hour or two at least. You owe me that much.'

'Let's go,' I said. 'Got a gun, Silver-Wig?'

'You know I'm not going. You know that. Please, please get out of here quickly.'

I stepped up close to her, almost pressing against her. 'You're going to stay here after turning me loose? Wait for that killer to come back so you can say so sorry? A man who kills like swatting a fly. Not much. You're going with me, Silver-Wig.'

'No.'

'Suppose,' I said, 'your handsome husband *did* kill Regan? Or suppose Canino did, without Eddie's knowing it. Just suppose. How long will *you* last, after turning me loose?'

'I'm not afraid of Canino. I'm still his boss's wife.'

'Eddie's a handful of mush,' I snarled. 'Canino would take him with a teaspoon. He'll take him the way the cat took the canary. A handful of mush. The only time a girl like you goes for a wrong gee is when he's a handful of mush.'

'Get out!' she almost spat at me.

'Okey.' I turned away from her and moved out through the half-open door into a dark hallway. Then she rushed after me and pushed past to the front door and opened it. She peered out into the wet blackness and listened. She motioned me forward.

'Good-bye,' she said under her breath. 'Good luck in everything but one thing. Eddie didn't kill Rusty Regan. You'll find him alive and well somewhere, when he wants to be found.'

I leaned against her and pressed her against the wall with my body. I pushed my mouth against her face. I talked to her that way.

'There's no hurry. All this was arranged in advance, rehearsed to the last detail, timed to the split second. Just like a radio programme. No hurry at all. Kiss me, Silver-Wig.'

Her face under my mouth was like ice. She put her hands up and took hold of my head and kissed me hard on the lips. Her lips were like ice, too.

I went out through the door and it closed behind me, without sound, and the rain blew in under the porch, not as cold as her lips.

29

The garage next door was dark. I crossed the gravel drive and a patch of sodden lawn. The road ran with small rivulets of water. It gurgled down a ditch on the far side. I had no hat. That must have fallen in the garage. Canino hadn't bothered to give it back to me. He hadn't thought I would need it any more. I imagined him driving back jauntily through the rain, alone, having left the gaunt and sulky Art and the probably stolen sedan in a safe place. She loved Eddie Mars and she was hiding to protect him. So he would find her there when he came back, calm beside the light and the untasted drink, and me tied up on the davenport. He would carry her stuff out to the car and go through the house carefully to make sure nothing incriminating was left. He would tell her to go out and wait. She wouldn't hear a shot. A blackjack is just as effective at short range. He would tell her he had left me tied up and I would get loose after a while. He would think she was that dumb. Nice Mr Canino.

The raincoat was open in front and I couldn't button it, being handcuffed. The skirts flapped against my legs like the wings of a large and tired bird. I came to the highway. Cars went by in a wide swirl of water illuminated by headlights. The tearing noise of their tyres died swiftly. I found my convertible where I had left it, both tyres fixed and mounted, so it could be driven away, if necessary. They thought of everything. I got into it and leaned down sideways under the wheel and fumbled aside the flap of leather that covered the pocket. I got the other gun, stuffed it up under my coat and started back. The world was small, shut in, black. A private world for Canino and me.

Half-way there the headlights nearly caught me. They turned swiftly off the highway and I slid down the bank into the wet ditch and flopped there breathing water. The car hummed by without slowing. I lifted my head, heard the rasp of its tyres as it left the road and took the gravel of the driveway. The motor died, the lights died, a door slammed. I didn't hear the house door shut, but a fringe of light trickled through the clump of trees, as though a shade had been moved aside from a window, or the light had been put on in the hall.

I came back to the soggy grass plot and sloshed across it. The car was between me and the house, the gun was down at my side, pulled as far around as I could get it, without pulling my left arm out by the roots. The car was dark, empty, warm. Water gurgled pleasantly in the radiator. I peered in at the door. The keys hung on the dash. Canino was very sure of himself. I went around the car and walked carefully across the gravel to the window and listened. I couldn't hear any voices, any sound but the swift bong-bong of the raindrops hitting the metal elbows at the bottom of the rain gutters.

I kept on listening. No loud voices, everything quiet and refined. He would be purring at her and she would be telling him she had let me go and I had promised to let them get away. He wouldn't believe me, as I wouldn't believe him. So he wouldn't be in there long. He would be on his way and take her with him. All I had to do was wait for him to come out.

I couldn't do it. I shifted the gun to my left hand and leaned down to scoop up a handful of gravel. I tossed it against the screen of the window. It was a feeble effort. Very little of it reached the glass above the screen, but the loose rattle of that little was like a dam bursting.

I ran back to the car and got on the running board behind it. The house had already gone dark. That was all. I dropped quietly on the running board and waited. No soap. Canino was too cagey.

I straightened up and got into the car backwards, fumbled around for the ignition key and turned it. I reached with my foot, but the starter button had to be on the dash. I found it at last, pulled it and the starter ground. The warm motor caught at once. It purred softly, contentedly. I got out of the car again and crouched down by the rear wheels.

I was shivering now but I knew Canino wouldn't like that last effect. He needed that car badly. A darkened window slid down inch by inch, only some shifting of light on the glass showing it moved. Flame spouted from it abruptly, the blended roar of three swift shots. Glass starred in the coupé. I yelled with agony. The yell went off into a wailing groan. The groan became a wet gurgle, choked with blood. I let the gurgle die sickeningly, on a choked gasp. It was nice work. I liked it. Canino liked it very much. I heard him laugh. It was a large booming laugh, not at all like the purr of his speaking voice.

Then silence for a little while, except for the rain and the quietly throbbing motor of the car. Then the house door crawled open, a deeper blackness in the black night. A figure showed in it cautiously, something white around the neck. It was her collar. She came out on the porch stiffly, a wooden woman. I caught the pale shine of her silver wig. Canino came crouched methodically behind her. It was so deadly it was almost funny.

She came down the steps. Now I could see the white stiffness of her face. She started towards the car. A bulwark of defence for Canino, in case I could still spit in his eye. Her voice spoke through the lisp of the rain, saying slowly, without any tone: 'I can't see a thing, Lash. The windows are misted.'

He grunted something and the girl's body jerked hard, as though he had jammed a gun into her back. She came on again and drew near the lightless car. I could see him behind her now, his hat, a side of his face, the bulk of his shoulder. The girl stopped rigid and screamed. A beautiful thin tearing scream that rocked me like a left hook.

'I can see him!' she screamed. 'Through the window. Behind the wheel, Lash!'

He fell for it like a bucket of lead. He knocked her roughly to one side and jumped forward, throwing his hand up. Three more spurts of flame cut the darkness. More glass scarred. One bullet went on through and smacked into a tree on my side. A ricochet whined off into the distance. But the motor went quietly on.

He was low down, crouched against the gloom, his face a greyness without form that seemed to come back slowly after the glare of the shots. If it was a revolver he had, it might be empty. It might not. He had fired six times, but he might have reloaded inside the house. I hoped he had. I didn't want him with an empty gun. But it might be an automatic.

I said: 'Finished?'

He whirled at me. Perhaps it would have been nice to allow him another shot or two, just like a gentleman of the old school. But his gun was still up and I couldn't wait any longer. Not long enough to be a gentleman of the old school. I shot him four times, the Colt straining against my ribs. The gun jumped out of his hand as if it had been kicked. He reached both his hands for his stomach. I could hear them smack hard against his body. He fell like that, straight forward, holding himself together with his broad hands. He fell face down in the wet gravel. And after that there wasn't a sound from him.

Silver-Wig didn't make a sound either. She stood rigid, with the rain swirling at her. I walked around Canino and kicked his gun, without any purpose. Then I walked after it and bent over sideways and picked it up. That put me close beside her. She spoke moodily, as if she was talking to herself.

'I – I was afraid you'd come back.'

I said: 'We had a date. I told you it was all arranged.' I began to laugh like a loon.

Then she was bending down over him, touching him. And after a little while she stood up with a small key on a thin chain.

She said bitterly: 'Did you have to kill him?'

I stopped laughing as suddenly as I had started. She went behind me and unlocked the handcuffs.

'Yes,' she said softly. 'I suppose you did.'

30

This was another day and the sun was shining again.

Captain Gregory of the Missing Persons Bureau looked heavily out of his office window at the barred upper floor of the Hall of Justice, white and clean after the rain. Then he turned ponderously in his swivel chair and tamped his pipe with a heat-scarred thumb and stared at me bleakly.

'So you got yourself in another jam.'

'Oh, you heard about it.'

'Brother, I sit here all day on my fanny and I don't look as if I had a brain in my head. But you'd be surprised what I hear. Shooting this Canino was all right I guess, but I don't figure the homicide boys pinned any medals on you.'

'There's been a lot of killings going on around me,' I said. 'I haven't been getting my share of it.'

He smiled patiently. 'Who told you this girl out there was Eddie Mars's wife?'

I told him. He listened carefully and yawned. He tapped his gold-studded mouth with a palm like a tray. 'I guess you figure I ought to have found her.'

'That's a fair deduction.'

'Maybe I knew,' he said. 'Maybe I thought if Eddie and

his woman wanted to play a little game like that, it would be smart – or as smart as I ever get – to let them think they were getting away with it. And then again maybe you think I was letting Eddie get away with it for more personal reasons.' He held his big hand out and revolved the thumb against the index and second fingers.

'No,' I said. 'I didn't really think that. Not even when Eddie seemed to know all about our talk here the other day.'

He raised his eyebrows as if raising them was an effort, a trick he was out of practice on. It furrowed his whole forehead and when it smoothed out it was full of white lines that turned reddish as I watched them.

'I'm a copper,' he said. 'Just a plain ordinary copper. Reasonably honest. As honest as you could expect a man to be in a world where it's out of style. That's mainly why I asked you to come in this morning. I'd like you to believe that. Being a copper I like to see the law win. I'd like to see the flashy well-dressed mugs like Eddie Mars spoiling their manicures in the rock quarry at Folsom, alongside of the poor little slum-bred hard guys that got knocked over on their first caper and never had a break since. That's what I'd like. You and me both lived too long to think I'm likely to see it happen. Not in this town, not in any town half this size, in any part of this wide, green and beautiful USA. We just don't run our country that way.'

I didn't say anything. He blew smoke with a backward jerk of his head, looked at the mouthpiece of his pipe and went on:

'But that don't mean I think Eddie Mars bumped off Regan or had any reason to or would have done it if he had. I just figured maybe he knows something about it, and maybe sooner or later something will sneak out into the open. Hiding his wife out at Realito was childish, but it's the kind of childishness a smart monkey thinks is smart. I had him in here last night, after the DA got through with him. He admitted the whole thing. He said he knew Canino as a reliable protection guy and that's what he had him for. He didn't know anything about his hobbies or want to. He didn't know Harry Jones. He didn't know Joe Brody. He did know Geiger, of course, but claims he didn't know about his racket. I guess you heard all that.'

'Yes.'

'You played it smart down there at Realito, brother. Not trying to cover up. We keep a file on unidentified bullets nowadays. Some day you might use that gun again. Then you'd be over a barrel.'

'I played it smart,' I said, and leered at him.

He knocked his pipe out and stared down at it broodingly. 'What happened to the girl?' he asked, not looking up.

'I don't know. They didn't hold her. We made statements, three sets of them, for Wilde, for the Sheriff's office, for the Homicide Bureau. They turned her loose. I haven't seen her since. I don't expect to.'

'Kind of a nice girl, they say. Wouldn't be one to play dirty games.'

'Kind of a nice girl,' I said.

Captain Gregory sighed and rumpled his mousy hair. 'There's just one more thing,' he said almost gently. 'You look like a nice guy, but you play too rough. If you really want to help the Sternwood family – leave 'em alone.'

'I think you're right, Captain.'

'How you feel?'

'Swell,' I said. 'I was standing on various pieces of carpet most of the night, being bawled out. Before that I got soaked to the skin and beaten up. I'm in perfect condition.'

'What the hell did you expect, brother?'

'Nothing else.' I stood up and grinned at him and started for the door. When I had almost reached it he cleared his throat suddenly and said in a harsh voice: 'I'm wasting my breath, huh? You still think you can find Regan.'

I turned round and looked him straight in the eyes. 'No, I don't think I can find Regan. I'm not even going to try. Does that suit you?'

He nodded slowly. Then he shrugged. 'I don't know what the hell I even said that for. Good luck, Marlowe. Drop around any time.'

'Thanks, Captain.'

I went down out of the City Hall and got my car from the parking lot and drove home to the Hobart Arms. I lay down on the bed with my coat off and stared at the ceiling and listened to the traffic sounds on the street outside and watched the sun move slowly across a corner of the ceiling. I tried to go to sleep, but sleep didn't come. I got up and took a drink, although it was the wrong time of day, and lay down again. I still couldn't go to sleep. My brain ticked like a clock. I sat up on the side of the bed and stuffed a pipe and said out loud:

'That old buzzard knows something.'

The pipe tasted as bitter as lye. I put it aside and lay down again. My mind drifted through waves of false memory, in which I seemed to do the same thing over and over again, go to the same places, meet the same people, say the same words to them, over and over again, and yet each time it seemed real, like something actually happening, and for the first time. I was driving hard along the highway through the rain, with Silver-Wig in the corner of the car, saying nothing, so that by the time we reached Los Angeles we seemed to be utter strangers again. I was getting out at an all-night drugstore and phoning Bernie Ohls that I had killed a man at Realito and was on my way over to Wilde's house with Eddie Mars's wife, who had seen me do it. I was pushing the car along the silent, rain-polished streets of Lafayette Park and up under the *porte-cochère* of Wilde's big frame house and the porch light was already on, Ohls having telephoned ahead that I was coming. I was in Wilde's study and he was behind his desk in a flowered dressing-gown and a tight hard face and a dappled cigar moved in his fingers and up to the bitter smile on his lips. Ohls was there and a slim grey scholarly man from the Sheriff's office who looked and talked more like a professor of economics than a cop. I was telling the story and they were listening quietly and Silver-Wig sat in a shadow with her hands folded in her lap, looking at nobody. There was a lot of telephoning.

There were two men from the Homicide Bureau who looked at me as if I was some kind of strange beast escaped from a travelling circus. I was driving again, with one of them beside me, to the Fulwider Building. We were there in the room where Harry Jones was still in the chair behind the desk, the twisted stiffness of his dead face and the sour-sweet smell in the room. There was a medical examiner, very young and husky, with red bristles on his neck. There was a fingerprint man fussing around and I was telling him not to forget the latch of the transom. (He found Canino's thumb print on it, the only print the brown man had left to back up my story.)

I was back again at Wilde's house, signing a typewritten statement his secretary had run off in another room. Then the door opened and Eddie Mars came in and an abrupt smile flashed to his face when he saw Silver-Wig, and he said: 'Hello, sugar', and she didn't look at him or answer him. Eddie Mars fresh and cheerful, in a dark business suit, with a fringed white scarf hanging outside his tweed overcoat. Then they were gone, everybody was gone out of the room but myself and Wilde, and Wilde was saying in a cold, angry voice: 'This is the last time, Marlowe. The next fast one you pull I'll throw you to the lions, no matter whose heart it breaks.'

It was like that, over and over again, lying on the bed and watching the patch of sunlight slide down the corner of the wall. Then the phone rang, and it was Norris, the Sternwood butler, with his usual untouchable voice.

'Mr Marlowe? I telephoned your office without success, so I took the liberty of trying to reach you at home.'

‘I was out most of the night,’ I said. ‘I haven’t been down.’

‘Yes, sir. The General would like to see you this morning, Mr Marlowe, if it’s convenient.’

‘Half an hour or so,’ I said. ‘How is he?’

‘He’s in bed, sir, but not doing badly.’

‘Wait till he sees me,’ I said, and hung up.

I shaved, changed clothes and started for the door. Then I went back and got Carmen’s little pearl-handled revolver and dropped it into my pocket. The sunlight was so bright that it danced. I got to the Sternwood place in twenty minutes and drove up under the arch at the side door. It was eleven-fifteen. The birds in the ornamental trees were crazy with song after the rain, the terraced lawns were as green as the Irish flag, and the whole estate looked as though it had been made about ten minutes before. I rang the bell. It was five days since I had rung it for the first time. It felt like a year.

A maid opened the door and led me along a side hall to the main hallway and left me there, saying Mr Norris would be down in a moment. The main hallway looked just the same. The portrait over the mantel had the same hot black eyes and the knight in the stained-glass window still wasn’t getting anywhere untying the naked damsel from the tree.

In a few minutes Norris appeared, and he hadn’t changed either. His acid-blue eyes were as remote as ever, his greyish-pink skin looked healthy and rested, and he moved as if he was twenty years younger than he really was. I was the one who felt the weight of the years.

We went up the tiled staircase and turned the opposite way from Vivian's room. With each step the house seemed to grow larger and more silent. We reached a massive old door that looked as if it had come out of a church. Norris opened it softly and looked in. Then he stood aside and I went in past him across what seemed to be about a quarter of a mile of carpet to a huge canopied bed like the one Henry the Eighth died in.

General Sternwood was propped up on pillows. His bloodless hands were clasped on top of the sheet. They looked grey against it. His black eyes were still full of fight and the rest of his face still looked like the face of a corpse.

'Sit down, Mr Marlowe.' His voice sounded weary and a little stiff.

I pulled a chair close to him and sat down. All the windows were shut tight. The room was sunless at that hour. Awnings cut off what glare there might be from the sky. The air had the faint sweetish smell of old age.

He stared at me silently for a long minute. He moved a hand as if to prove to himself that he could still move it, then folded it back over the other. He said lifelessly:

'I didn't ask you to look for my son-in-law, Mr Marlowe.'

'You wanted me to, though.'

'I didn't ask you to. You assume a great deal. I usually ask for what I want.'

I didn't say anything.

'You have been paid,' he went on coldly. 'The money is of no consequence one way or the other. I merely feel that you have, no doubt unintentionally, betrayed a trust.'

He closed his eyes on that. I said: 'Is that all you wanted to see me about?'

He opened his eyes again, very slowly, as though the lids were made of lead. 'I suppose you are angry at that remark,' he said.

I shook my head. 'You have an advantage over me, General. It's an advantage I wouldn't want to take away from you, not a hair of it. It's not much, considering what you have to put up with. You can say anything you like to me and I wouldn't think of getting angry. I'd like to offer you your money back. It may mean nothing to you. It might mean something to me.'

'What does it mean to you?'

'It means I have refused payment for an unsatisfactory job. That's all.'

'Do you do many unsatisfactory jobs?'

'A few. Everyone does.'

'Why did you go to see Captain Gregory?'

I leaned back and hung an arm over the back of the chair. I studied his face. It told me nothing. I didn't know the answer to his question – no satisfactory answer.

I said: 'I was convinced you put those Geiger notes up to me chiefly as a test, and that you were a little afraid Regan might somehow be involved in an attempt to blackmail you. I didn't know anything about Regan then. It wasn't until I talked to Captain Gregory that I realized Regan wasn't that sort of guy in all probability.'

'That is scarcely answering my question.'

I nodded. 'No. That is scarcely answering your question. I guess I just don't like to admit that I played a hunch. The morning I was here, after I left you out in the orchid house, Mrs Regan sent for me. She seemed to assume I was hired to look for her husband and she didn't seem to like it. She let drop however that "they" had found his car in a certain garage. The "they" could only be the police. Consequently the police must know something about it. If they did, the Missing Persons Bureau would be the department that would have the case. I didn't know whether you had reported it, of course, or somebody else, or whether they had found the car through somebody reporting it abandoned in a garage. But I know cops, and I knew that if they got that much, they would get a little more – especially as your driver happened to have a police record. I didn't know how much more they would get. That started me thinking about the Missing Persons Bureau. What convinced me was something in Mr Wilde's manner the night we had the conference over at his house about Geiger and so on. We were alone for a minute and he asked me whether you had told me you were looking for Regan. I said you had told me you wished you knew where he was and that he was all right. Wilde pulled his lip in and looked funny. I knew just as plainly as though he had said it that by "looking for Regan" he meant using the machinery of the law to look for him. Even then I tried to go up against Captain Gregory in such a way that I wouldn't tell him anything he didn't know already.'

'And you allowed Captain Gregory to think I had employed you to find Rusty?'

'Yeah. I guess I did – when I was sure he had the case.'

He closed his eyes. They twitched a little. He spoke with them closed. 'And do you consider that ethical?'

'Yes,' I said. 'I do.'

The eyes opened again. The piercing blackness of them was startling coming suddenly out of that dead face. 'Perhaps I don't understand,' he said.

'Maybe you don't. The head of a Missing Persons Bureau isn't a talker. He wouldn't be in that office if he was. This one is a very smart cagey guy who tries, with a lot of success at first, to give the impression he's a middle-aged hack fed up with his job. The game I play is not spillikins. There's always a large element of bluff connected with it. Whatever I might say to a cop, he would be apt to discount it. And to *that* cop it wouldn't make much difference what I said. When you hire a boy in my line of work it isn't like hiring a window-washer and showing him eight windows and saying: "Wash those and you're through." *You* don't know what I have to go through or over or under to do your job for you. I do it my way. I do my best to protect you and I may break a few rules, but I break them in your favour. The client comes first, unless he's crooked. Even then all I do is hand the job back to him and keep my mouth shut. After all you didn't tell me *not* to go to Captain Gregory.'

'That would have been rather difficult,' he said with a faint smile.

'Well, what have I done wrong? Your man Norris seemed to think when Geiger was eliminated the case was over. I don't see it that way. Geiger's method of approach puzzled me and still does. I'm not Sherlock Holmes or

Philo Vance. I don't expect to go over ground the police have covered and pick up a broken pen point and build a case from it. If you think there is anybody in the detective business making a living doing that sort of thing, you don't know much about cops. It's not things like that they overlook if they overlook anything. I'm not saying they often overlook anything when they're really allowed to work. But if they do, it's apt to be something looser and vaguer, like a man of Geiger's type sending you his evidence of debt and asking you to pay like a gentleman – Geiger, a man in a shady racket, in a vulnerable position, protected by a racketeer and having at least some negative protection from some of the police. Why did he do that? Because he wanted to find out if there was anything putting pressure on you. If there was, you would pay him. If not, you would ignore him and wait for his next move. But there was something putting a pressure on you. Regan. You were afraid he was not what he had appeared to be, that he had stayed around and had been nice to you just long enough to find out how to play games with your bank account.'

He started to say something but I interrupted him. 'Even at that it wasn't your money you cared about. It wasn't even your daughters. You've more or less written them off. It's that you're still too proud to be played for a sucker – and you really liked Regan.'

There was a silence. Then the General said quietly: 'You talk too damn much, Marlowe. Am I to understand you are still trying to solve that puzzle?'

'No. I've quit. I've been warned off. The boys think

I play too rough. That's why I thought I should give you back your money – because it isn't a completed job by my standards.'

He smiled. 'Quit nothing,' he said. 'I'll pay you another thousand dollars to find Rusty. He doesn't have to come back. I don't even have to know where he is. A man has a right to live his own life. I don't blame him for walking out on my daughter, nor even for going so abruptly. It was probably a sudden impulse. I want to know that he is all right wherever he is. I want to know it from him directly, and if he should happen to need money, I should want him to have that also. Am I clear?'

I said: 'Yes, General.'

He rested a little while, lax on the bed, his eyes closed and dark-lidded, his mouth tight and bloodless. He was used up. He was pretty nearly licked. He opened his eyes again and tried to grin at me.

'I guess I'm a sentimental old goat,' he said. 'And no soldier at all. I took a fancy to that boy. He seemed pretty clean to me. I must be a little too vain about my judgment of character. Find him for me, Marlowe. Just find him.'

'I'll try,' I said. 'You'd better rest now. I've talked your arm off.'

I got up quickly and walked across the wide floor and out. He had his eyes shut again before I opened the door. His hands lay limp on the sheet. He looked a lot more like a dead man than most dead men look. I shut the door quietly and went back along the upper hall and down the stairs.

31

The butler appeared with my hat. I put it on and said: 'What do you think of him?'

'He's not as weak as he looks, sir.'

'If he was, he'd be ready for burial. What did this Regan fellow have that bored into him so?'

The butler looked at me levelly and yet with a queer lack of expression. 'Youth, sir,' he said. 'And the soldier's eye.'

'Like yours,' I said.

'If I may say so, sir, not unlike yours.'

'Thanks. How are the ladies this morning?'

He shrugged politely.

'Just what I thought,' I said, and he opened the door for me.

I stood outside on the step and looked down the vistas of grassed terraces and trimmed trees and flowerbeds to the tall metal railing at the bottom of the gardens. I saw Carmen about half-way down, sitting on a stone bench, with her head between her hands, looking forlorn and alone.

I went down the red brick steps that led from terrace to terrace. I was quite close before she heard me. She jumped up and whirled like a cat. She wore the light blue slacks she had worn the first time I saw her. Her blonde hair was the same loose tawny wave. Her face was white. Red spots flared in her cheeks as she looked at me. Her eyes were slaty.

'Bored?' I said.

She smiled slowly, rather shyly, then nodded quickly. Then she whispered: 'You're not mad at me?'

'I thought you were mad at me.'

She put her thumb up and giggled. 'I'm not.' When she giggled I didn't like her any more. I looked around. A target hung on a tree about thirty feet away, with some darts sticking to it. There were three or four more on the stone bench where she had been sitting.

'For people with money you and your sister don't seem to have much fun,' I said.

She looked at me under her long lashes. This was the look that was supposed to make me roll over on my back. I said: 'You like throwing those darts?'

'Uh-huh.'

'That reminds me of something.' I looked back towards the house. By moving about three feet I made a tree hide me from it. I took her little pearl-handled gun out of my pocket. 'I brought you back your artillery. I cleaned it and loaded it up. Take my tip – don't shoot it at people, unless you get to be a better shot. Remember?'

Her face went paler and her thin thumb dropped. She looked at me, then at the gun I was holding. There was a fascination in her eyes. 'Yes,' she said, and nodded. Then suddenly: 'Teach me to shoot.'

'Huh?'

'Teach me how to shoot. I'd like that.'

'Here? It's against the law.'

She came close to me and took the gun out of my hand, cuddled her hand around the butt. Then she tucked it quickly inside her slacks, almost with a furtive movement, and looked around.

'I know where,' she said in a secret voice. 'Down by some of the old wells.' She pointed off down the hill. 'Teach me?'

I looked into her slaty blue eyes. I might as well have looked at a couple of bottle-tops. 'All right. Give me back the gun until I see if the place looks all right.'

She smiled and made a mouth, then handed it back with a secret naughty air, as if she was giving me a key to her room. We walked up the steps and around to my car. The gardens seemed deserted. The sunshine was as empty as a head waiter's smile. We got into the car and I drove down the sunken driveway and out through the gates.

'Where's Vivian?' I asked.

'Not up yet.' She giggled.

I drove on down the hill through the quiet, opulent streets with their faces washed by the rain, bore east to La Brea, then south. We reached the place she meant in about ten minutes.

'In there.' She leaned out of the window and pointed.

It was a narrow dirt road, not much more than a track, like the entrance to some foothill ranch. A wide five-barred gate was folded back against a stump and looked as if it hadn't been shut in years. The road was fringed with tall eucalyptus trees and deeply rutted.

Trucks had used it. It was empty and sunny now, but not yet dusty. The rain had been too hard and too recent. I followed the ruts along and the noise of city traffic grew curiously and quickly faint, as if this were not in the city at all, but far away in a daydream land. Then the oil-stained, motionless walking-beam of a squat wooden derrick stuck up over a branch. I could see the rusty old steel cable that connected this walking-beam with half a dozen others. The beams didn't move, probably hadn't moved for a year. The wells were no longer pumping. There was a pile of rusted pipe, a loading platform that sagged at one end, half a dozen empty oil drums lying in a ragged pile. There was the stagnant, oil-scummed water of an old sump iridescent in the sunlight.

'Are they going to make a park of all this?' I asked.

She dipped her chin down and gleamed at me.

'It's about time. The smell of that sump would poison a herd of goats. This the place you had in mind?'

'Uh-huh. Like it?'

'It's beautiful.' I pulled up beside the loading platform. We got out. I listened. The hum of the traffic was a distant web of sound, like the buzzing of bees. The place was as lonely as a churchyard. Even after the rain the tall eucalyptus trees still looked dusty. They always look dusty. A branch broken off by the wind had fallen over the edge of the sump and the flat leathery leaves dangled in the water.

I walked around the sump and looked into the pump-house. There was some junk in it, nothing that looked like recent activity. Outside a big wooden bull wheel was tilted against the wall. It looked like a good place all right.

I went back to the car. The girl stood beside it preening her hair and holding it out in the sun. 'Gimme,' she said, and held her hand out.

I took the gun out and put it in her palm. I bent down and picked up a rusty can.

'Take it easy now,' I said. 'It's loaded in all five. I'll go over and set this can in that square opening in the middle of that big wooden wheel. See?' I pointed. She ducked her head, delighted. 'That's about thirty feet. Don't start shooting until I get back beside you. Okey?'

'Okey,' she giggled.

I went back around the sump and set the can up in the middle of the bull wheel. It made a swell target. If she missed the can, which she was certain to do, she would probably hit the wheel. That would stop a small slug completely. However, she wasn't going to hit even that.

I went back towards her around the sump. When I was about ten feet from her, at the edge of the sump, she showed me all her sharp little teeth and brought the gun up and started to hiss.

I stopped dead, the sump water stagnant and stinking at my back.

'Stand there, you son of a bitch,' she said.

The gun pointed at my chest. Her hand seemed to be quite steady. The hissing sound grew louder and her face had the scraped bone look. Aged, deteriorated, become animal, and not a nice animal.

I laughed at her. I started to walk towards her. I saw her small finger tighten on the trigger and grow white at the tip. I was about six feet away from her when she started to shoot.

The sound of the gun made a sharp slap, without body, a brittle crack in the sunlight. I didn't see any smoke. I stopped again and grinned at her.

She fired twice more, very quickly. I don't think any of the shots would have missed. There were five in the little gun. She had fired four. I rushed her.

I didn't want the last one in my face, so I swerved to one side. She gave it to me quite carefully, not worried at all. I think I felt the hot breath of the powder blast a little.

I straightened up. 'My, but you're cute,' I said.

Her hand holding the empty gun began to shake violently. The gun fell out of it. Her mouth began to shake. Her whole face went to pieces. Then her head screwed up towards her left ear and froth showed on her lips. Her breath made a whining sound. She swayed.

I caught her as she fell. She was already unconscious. I prised her teeth open with both hands and stuffed a wadded handkerchief in between them. It took all my strength to do it. I lifted her up and got her into the car, then went back for the gun and dropped it into my pocket. I climbed in under the wheel, backed the car and drove back the way we had come along the rutted road, out of the gateway, back up the hill and so home.

Carmen lay crumpled in the corner of the car, without motion. I was half-way up the drive to the house before she stirred. Then her eyes suddenly opened wide and wild. She sat up.

'What happened?' she gasped.

'Nothing. Why?'

'Oh, yes it did,' she giggled. 'I wet myself.'

'They always do,' I said.

She looked at me with a sudden sick speculation and began to moan.

32

The gentle-eyed, horse-faced maid let me into the long grey and white upstairs sitting-room with the ivory drapes tumbled extravagantly on the floor and the white carpet from wall to wall. A screen star's boudoir, a place of charm and seduction, artificial as a wooden leg. It was empty at the moment. The door closed behind me with the unnatural softness of a hospital door. A breakfast table on wheels stood by the chaise-longue. Its silver glittered. There were cigarette ashes in the coffee cup. I sat down and waited.

It seemed a long time before the door opened again and Vivian came in. She was in oyster-white lounging pyjamas trimmed with white fur, cut as flowingly as a summer sea frothing on the beach of some small and exclusive island.

She went past me in long smooth strides and sat down on the edge of the chaise-longue. There was a cigarette in her lips, at the corner of her mouth. Her nails to-day were copper red from quick to tip, without half-moons.

'So you're just a brute after all,' she said quietly, staring at me. 'An utter callous brute. You killed a man last night. Never mind how I heard it. I heard it. And now you have to come out here and frighten my kid sister into a fit.'

I didn't say a word. She began to fidget. She moved over to a slipper chair and put her head back against a white cushion that lay along the back of the chair against the wall. She blew pale grey smoke upwards and watched it float towards the ceiling and come apart in wisps that were for a little while distinguishable from the air and then melted and were nothing. Then very slowly she lowered her eyes and gave me a cool hard glance.

'I don't understand you,' she said. 'I'm thankful as hell one of us kept his head the night before last. It's bad enough to have a bootlegger in my past. Why don't you for Christ's sake say something?'

'How is she?'

'Oh, she's all right, I suppose. Fast asleep. She always goes to sleep. What did you do to her?'

'Not a thing. I came out of the house after seeing your father and she was out in front. She had been throwing darts at a target on a tree. I went down to speak to her because I had something that belonged to her. A little revolver Owen Taylor gave her once. She took it over to Brody's place the other evening, the evening he was killed. I had to take it away from her there. I didn't mention it, so perhaps you didn't know it.'

The black Sternwood eyes got large and empty. It was her turn not to say anything.

'She was pleased to get her little gun back and she

wanted me to teach her how to shoot and she wanted to show me the old oil wells down the hill where your family made some of its money. So we went down there and the place was pretty creepy, all rusted metal and old wood and silent wells and greasy scummy sumps. Maybe that upset her. I guess you've been there yourself. It was kind of eerie.'

'Yes – it is.' It was a small breathless voice now.

'So we went in there and I stuck a can up in a bull wheel for her to pop at. She threw a wingding. Looked like a mild epileptic fit to me.'

'Yes.' The same minute voice. 'She has them once in a while. Is that all you wanted to see me about?'

'I guess you still wouldn't tell me what Eddie Mars has on you.'

'Nothing at all. And I'm getting a little tired of that question,' she said coldly.

'Do you know a man named Canino?'

She drew her fine black brows together in thought. 'Vaguely. I seem to remember the name.'

'Eddie Mars's trigger man. A tough hombre, they said. I guess he was. Without a little help from a lady I'd be where he is – in the morgue.'

'The ladies seem to –.' She stopped dead and whitened. 'I can't joke about it,' she said simply.

'I'm not joking, and if I seem to talk in circles, it just seems that way. It all ties together – everything. Geiger and his cute little blackmail tricks, Brody and his pictures, Eddie Mars and his roulette tables, Canino and the girl Rusty Regan didn't run away with. It all ties together.'

'I'm afraid I don't even know what you're talking about.'

'Suppose you did – it would be something like this. Geiger got his hooks into your sister, which isn't very difficult, and got some notes from her and tried to blackmail your father with them, in a nice way. Eddie Mars was behind Geiger, protecting him and using him for a cat's-paw. Your father sent for me instead of paying up, which showed he wasn't scared about anything. Eddie Mars wanted to know that. He had something on you and he wanted to know if he had it on the General too. If he had, he could collect a lot of money in a hurry. If not, he would have to wait until you got your share of the family fortune, and in the meantime be satisfied with whatever spare cash he could take away from you across the roulette table. Geiger was killed by Owen Taylor, who was in love with your silly little sister and didn't like the kind of games Geiger played with her. That didn't mean anything to Eddie. He was playing a deeper game than Geiger knew anything about, or than Brody knew anything about, or anybody except you and Eddie and a tough guy named Canino. Your husband disappeared and Eddie, knowing everybody knew there had been bad blood between him and Regan, hid his wife out at Realito and put Canino to guard her, so that it would look as if she had run away with Regan. He even got Regan's car into the garage of the place where Mona Mars had been living. But that sounds a little silly taken merely as an attempt to divert suspicion that Eddie had killed your husband or had him killed. It isn't so silly, really. He had another motive. He was playing for a million or so. He knew where Regan had gone and why and he didn't want the police to have to find out. He wanted them to have an explanation of the disappearance that would keep them satisfied. Am I boring you?'

'You tire me,' she said in a dead, exhausted voice. 'God, how you tire me!'

'I'm sorry. I'm not just fooling around trying to be clever. Your father offered me a thousand dollars this morning to find Regan. That's a lot of money to me, but I can't do it.'

Her mouth jumped open. Her breath was suddenly strained and harsh. 'Give me a cigarette,' she said thickly. 'Why?' The pulse in her throat had begun to throb.

I gave her a cigarette and lit a match and held it for her. She drew in a lungful of smoke and let it out raggedly and then the cigarette seemed to be forgotten between her fingers. She never drew on it again.

'Well, the Missing Persons Bureau can't find him,' I said. 'It's not so easy. What they can't do it's not likely that I can do.'

'Oh.' There was a shade of relief in her voice.

'That's one reason. The Missing Persons people think he just disappeared on purpose, pulled down the curtain, as they call it. They don't think Eddie Mars did away with him.'

'Who said anybody did away with him?'

'We're coming to it,' I said.

For a brief instant her face seemed to come to pieces, to become merely a set of features without form or control. Her mouth looked like the prelude to a scream. But only for an instant. The Sternwood blood had to be good for something more than her black eyes and her recklessness.

I stood up and took the smoking cigarette from between her fingers and killed it in an ashtray. Then I took Carmen's little gun out of my pocket and laid it carefully, with exaggerated care, on her white satin knee. I balanced it there, and stepped back with my head on one side like a window-dresser getting the effect of a new twist of a scarf around a dummy's neck.

I sat down again. She didn't move. Her eyes came down millimetre by millimetre and looked at the gun.

'It's harmless,' I said. 'All five chambers empty. She fired them all. She fired them all at me.'

The pulse jumped wildly in her throat. Her voice tried to say something and couldn't. She swallowed.

'From a distance of five or six feet,' I said. 'Cute little thing, isn't she? Too bad I had loaded the gun with blanks.' I grinned nastily. 'I had a hunch about what she would do – if she got the chance.'

She brought her voice back from a long way off. 'You're a horrible man,' she said. 'Horrible.'

'Yeah. You're her big sister. What are you going to do about it?'

'You can't prove a word of it.'

'Can't prove what?'

'That she fired at you. You said you were down there around the wells with her, alone. You can't prove a word of what you say.'

'Oh that,' I said. 'I wasn't thinking of trying. I was thinking of another time – when the shells in the little gun had bullets in them.'

Her eyes were pools of darkness, much emptier than darkness.

'I was thinking of the day Regan disappeared,' I said. 'Late in the afternoon. When he took her down to those old wells to teach her to shoot and put up a can somewhere and told her to pop at it and stood near her while she shot. And she didn't shoot at the can. She turned the gun and shot him, just the way she tried to shoot me to-day, and for the same reason.'

She moved a little and the gun slid off her knee and fell to the floor. It was one of the loudest sounds I ever heard. Her eyes were riveted on my face. Her voice was a stretched whisper of agony. 'Carmen . . . Merciful God, Carmen! . . . Why?'

'Do I really have to tell you why she shot at me?'

'Yes.' Her eyes were still terrible. 'I'm – I'm afraid you do.'

'Night before last when I got home she was in my apartment. She'd kidded the manager into letting her in to wait for me. She was in my bed – naked. I threw her out on her ear. I guess maybe Regan did the same thing to her some time. But you can't do that to Carmen.'

She drew her lips back and made a half-hearted attempt to lick them. It made her, for a brief instant, look like a frightened child. The lines of her cheeks sharpened and her hand went up slowly like an artificial hand worked by wires and its fingers closed slowly and stiffly around the white fur at her collar. They drew the fur tight against her throat. After that she just sat staring.

'Money,' she croaked. 'I suppose you want money.'

'How much money?' I tried not to sneer.

'Fifteen thousand dollars?'

I nodded. 'That would be about right. That would be the established fee. That was what he had in his pockets when she shot him. That would be what Mr Canino got for disposing of the body when you went to Eddie Mars for help. But that would be small change to what Eddie expects to collect one of these days, wouldn't it?'

'You son of a bitch!' she said.

'Uh-huh. I'm a very smart guy. I haven't a feeling or a scruple in the world. All I have the itch for is money. I am so money greedy that for twenty-five bucks a day and expenses, mostly gasolene and whisky, I do my thinking myself, what there is of it: I risk my whole future, the hatred of the cops and of Eddie Mars and his pals, I dodge bullets and eat saps, and say thank you very much, if you have any more trouble, I hope you'll think of me, I'll just leave one of my cards in case anything comes up. I do all this for twenty-five bucks a day – and maybe just a little to protect what little pride a broken and sick old man has left in his blood, in the thought that his blood is not poison, and that although his two little girls are a trifle wild, as many nice girls are these days, they are not perverts or killers. And that makes me a son of a bitch. All right. I don't care anything about that. I've been called that by people of all sizes and shapes, including your little sister. She called me worse than that for not getting into bed with her. I got five hundred dollars from your father, which I didn't ask for, but he can afford to give it to me. I can get another thousand for finding Mr Rusty Regan, if I could find him. Now you offer me fifteen grand. That makes me a big shot. With fifteen grand I could own a home and a new car and four suits of clothes. I might even take a vacation without worrying about losing a case. That's fine. What are you offering it to me for? Can I go on being a son of a bitch, or do I have to become a gentleman, like that lush that passed out in his car the other night?'

She was as silent as a stone woman.

'All right,' I went on heavily. 'Will you take her away? Somewhere far off from here where they can handle her type, where they will keep guns and knives and fancy drinks away from her? Hell, she might even get herself cured, you know. It's been done.'

She got up and walked slowly to the windows. The drapes lay in heavy ivory folds beside her feet. She stood among the folds and looked out, towards the quiet darkish foothills. She stood motionless, almost blending into the drapes. Her hands hung loose at her sides. Utterly motionless hands. She turned and came back along the room and walked past me blindly. When she was behind me she caught her breath sharply and spoke.

'He's in the sump,' she said. 'A horrible decayed thing. I did it. I did just what you said. I went to Eddie Mars. She came home and told me about it, just like a child. She's not normal. I knew the police would get it all out of her. In a little while she would even brag about it. And if Dad knew, he would call them instantly and tell them the whole story. And some time in that night he would die. It's not his dying – it's what he would be thinking just before he died. Rusty wasn't a bad fellow. I didn't love him. He was all right, I guess. He just didn't mean anything to me, one way or another, alive or dead, compared with keeping it from Dad.'

'So you let her run around loose,' I said, 'getting into other jams.'

'I was playing for time. Just for time. I played the wrong way, of course. I thought she might even forget it herself. I've heard they do forget what happens in those fits. Maybe she has forgotten it. I knew Eddie Mars would bleed me white, but I didn't care. I had to have help and I could only get it from somebody like him . . . There have been times when I hardly believed it all myself. And other times when I had to get drunk quickly – whatever time of day it was. Awfully damn quickly.'

'You'll take her away,' I said. 'And do that awfully damn quickly.'

She still had her back to me. She said softly now: 'What about you?'

'Nothing about me. I'm leaving. I'll give you three days. If you're gone by then – okey. If you're not, out it comes. And don't think I don't mean that.'

She turned suddenly. 'I don't know what to say to you. I don't know how to begin.'

'Yeah. Get her out of here and see that she's watched every minute. Promise?'

'I promise. Eddie –'

'Forget Eddie. I'll go see him after I get some rest. I'll handle Eddie.'

'He'll try to kill you.'

'Yeah,' I said. 'His best boy couldn't. I'll take a chance on the others. Does Norris know?'

'He'll never tell.'

'I thought he knew.'

I went quickly away from her down the room and out and down the tiled staircase to the front hall. I didn't see anybody when I left. I found my hat alone this time. Outside the bright gardens had a haunted look, as though small wild eyes were watching me from behind the bushes, as though the sunshine itself had a mysterious something in its light. I got into my car and drove off down the hill.

What did it matter where you lay once you were dead? In a dirty sump or in a marble tower on top of a high hill? You were dead, you were sleeping the big sleep, you were not bothered by things like that. Oil and water were the same as wind and air to you. You just slept the big sleep, not caring about the nastiness of how you died or where you fell. Me, I was part of the nastiness now. Far more a part of it than Rusty Regan was. But the old man didn't have to be. He could lie quiet in his canopied bed, with his bloodless hands folded on the sheet, waiting. His heart was a brief, uncertain murmur. His thoughts were as grey as ashes. And in a little while he too, like Rusty Regan, would be sleeping the big sleep.

*

On the way downtown I stopped at a bar and had a couple of double Scotches. They didn't do me any good. All they did was make me think of Silver-Wig, and I never saw her again.

PENGUIN CLASSICS

THE HOUSE OF THE DEAD
FYODOR DOSTOYEVSKY

'Here was the house of the living dead, a life like none other upon earth'

In January 1850 Dostoyevsky was sent to a remote Siberian prison camp for his part in a political conspiracy. The four years he spent there, startlingly re-created in *The House of the Dead*, were the most agonizing of his life. In this fictionalized account he recounts his soul-destroying incarceration through the cool, detached tones of his narrator, Aleksandr Petrovich Goryanchikov: the daily battle for survival, the wooden plank beds, the cabbage soup swimming with cockroaches, his strange 'family' of boastful, ugly, cruel convicts. Yet *The House of the Dead* is far more than a work of documentary realism: it is also a powerful novel of redemption, describing one man's spiritual and moral death and the miracle of his gradual reawakening.

This edition includes an introduction and notes by David McDuff discussing the circumstances of Dostoyevsky's imprisonment, the origins of the novel in his prison writings and the character of Aleksandr Petrovich.

Translated with an introduction and notes by David McDuff

PENGUIN CLASSICS

THE IDIOT
FYODOR DOSTOYEVSKY

'He's simple-minded, but he has all his wits about him, in the most noble sense of the word, of course'

Returning to St Petersburg from a Swiss sanatorium, the gentle and naive Prince Myshkin – known as 'the idiot' – pays a visit to his distant relative General Yepanchin and proceeds to charm the General, his wife and his three daughters. But his life is thrown into turmoil when he chances on a photograph of the beautiful Nastasya Filippovna. Utterly infatuated with her, he soon finds himself caught up in a love triangle and drawn into a web of blackmail, betrayal and, finally, murder. In Prince Myshkin, Dosteyevsky set out to portray the purity of 'a truly beautiful soul' and to explore the perils that innocence and goodness face in a corrupt world.

David McDuff's major new translation brilliantly captures the novel's idiosyncratic and dream-like language and the nervous, elliptic flow of the narrative. This edition also includes an introduction by William Mills Todd III, further reading, a chronology of Dostoyevsky's life and work, a note on the translation and explanatory notes.

Translated by David McDuff with an introduction by William Mills Todd III

PENGUIN CLASSICS

NOTES FROM UNDERGROUND *AND* THE DOUBLE
FYODOR DOSTOYEVSKY

'It is best to do nothing! The best thing is conscious inertia!
So long live the underground!'

Alienated from society and paralysed by a sense of his own insignificance, the anonymous narrator of Dostoyevsky's groundbreaking *Notes from Underground* tells the story of his tortured life. With bitter sarcasm, he describes his refusal to become a worker in the 'ant-hill' of society and his gradual withdrawal to an existence 'underground'. The seemingly ordinary world of St Petersburg takes on a nightmarish quality in *The Double* when a government clerk encounters a man who exactly resembles him – his double perhaps, or possibly the darker side of his own personality. Like *Notes from Underground*, this is a masterly study of human consciousness.

Jessie Coulson's introduction discusses the critical reception of the stories and the themes they share with Dostoyevksy's great novels.

'*Notes from Underground*, with its mood of intellectual irony and alienation, can be seen as the first modern novel … That sense of the meaningless of existence that runs through much of twentieth-century writing – from Conrad and Kafka, to Beckett and beyond – starts in Dostoyevsky's work' Malcolm Bradbury

Translated with an introduction by Jessie Coulson

PENGUIN CLASSICS

DEAD SOULS
NIKOLAI GOGOL

'It's not a question of the living. I've nothing to do with them.
I'm asking for the dead'

Chichikov, a mysterious stranger, arrives in the provincial town of 'N', visiting a succession of landowners and making each a strange offer. He proposes to buy the names of dead serfs still registered on the census, saving their owners from paying tax on them, and to use these 'souls' as collateral to re-invent himself as a gentleman. In this ebullient masterpiece, Gogol created a grotesque gallery of human types, from the bear-like Sobakevich to the insubstantial fool Manilov, and, above all, the devilish conman Chichikov. *Dead Souls*, Russia's first major novel, is one of the most unusual works of nineteenth-century fiction and a devastating satire on social hypocrisy.

David Magarshack's introduction discusses Gogol's plan for a novel in three parts, tracing Chichikov's progress from sin to redemption, and tells how Gogol destroyed part of the manuscript in the grip of madness. The surviving sections, volume one and a fragment of volume two, are translated here.

'Gogol was a strange creature, but then genius is always strange'
Vladimir Nabokov

Translated with an introduction by David Magarshack

PENGUIN CLASSICS

A HERO OF OUR TIME
MIKHAIL LERMONTOV

'I'm still in love with her … I'd give my life for her. But she bores me'

Proud, wilful and intensely charismatic, Pechorin is bored by the stifling world that envelops him. With a predatory energy for any activity that will relieve his ennui, he embarks on a series of adventures – encountering smugglers, brigands, soldiers, lovers and rivals – and leaves a trail of broken hearts behind him. With its cynical, immoral hero, Lermontov's novel outraged many critics when it was published in 1840. Yet it was also a literary landmark: an acutely observed psychological novel, narrated from a number of different perspectives, through which the true and complex nature of Pechorin slowly emerges.

Paul Foote's fine translation is accompanied by an introduction discussing the figure of Pechorin within the literary tradition of 'superfluous men' and the novel's influence on Tolstoy, Dostoyevsky and Chekhov. The edition also includes a chronology, explanatory notes and a historical note on the Caucasus.

'Vigorous and audacious … it retains its power as a psychological study'
Julian Barnes

Translated with an introduction by Paul Foote